Dynamite . . .

As he stepped outside, the ground shook hard enough to cause Slocum to stagger. He caught himself against the edge of the bunkhouse in time to brace for another huge explosion. Before the last of the thunder had died away, Slocum was running for the mouth of the Silver Emperor Mine. Huge clouds of dust billowed from deep within the mine, followed quickly by the sound of rock *tearing* . . .

JAKE LOGAN

SLOCUM
AND THE
MOJAVE GUNS

J

JOVE BOOKS, NEW YORK

THE BERKLEY PUBLISHING GROUP
Published by the Penguin Group
Penguin Group (USA) Inc.
375 Hudson Street, New York, New York 10014, USA
Penguin Group (Canada), 90 Eglinton Avenue East, Suite 700, Toronto, Ontario M4P 2Y3, Canada
(a division of Pearson Penguin Canada Inc.)
Penguin Books Ltd., 80 Strand, London WC2R 0RL, England
Penguin Group Ireland, 25 St. Stephen's Green, Dublin 2, Ireland (a division of Penguin Books Ltd.)
Penguin Group (Australia), 250 Camberwell Road, Camberwell, Victoria 3124, Australia
(a division of Pearson Australia Group Pty. Ltd.)
Penguin Books India Pvt. Ltd., 11 Community Centre, Panchsheel Park, New Delhi—110 017, India
Penguin Group (NZ), Cnr. Airborne and Rosedale Roads, Albany, Auckland 1310, New Zealand
(a division of Pearson New Zealand Ltd.)
Penguin Books (South Africa) (Pty.) Ltd., 24 Sturdee Avenue, Rosebank, Johannesburg 2196,
South Africa

Penguin Books Ltd., Registered Offices: 80 Strand, London WC2R 0RL, England

This is a work of fiction. Names, characters, places, and incidents either are the product of the author's imagination or are used fictitiously, and any resemblance to actual persons, living or dead, business establishments, events, or locales is entirely coincidental.

SLOCUM AND THE MOJAVE GUNS

A Jove Book / published by arrangement with the author

PRINTING HISTORY
Jove edition / January 2006

Copyright © 2006 by The Berkley Publishing Group.

ISBN: 0-515-14054-6

JOVE®
Jove Books are published by The Berkley Publishing Group,
a division of Penguin Group (USA) Inc.,
375 Hudson Street, New York, New York 10014.
JOVE is a registered trademark of Penguin Group (USA) Inc.
The "J" design is a trademark belonging to Penguin Group (USA) Inc.

PRINTED IN THE UNITED STATES OF AMERICA

10 9 8 7 6 5 4 3 2 1

1

"Heat's enough to render you down to a nuthin' more 'n a boilin' puddle o' lard in a thrice," the driver called back to John Slocum. Slocum tugged at the broad brim of his Stetson to keep the morning sun from his eyes. He didn't have to be told it was hot, damned hot, out here in the middle of Death Valley. The sun was barely poking up above the Amargosa Mountains and already he was feeling sticky under the collar.

"Yep, Zeb, surely is," said the shotgun guard riding beside him on the hard wood bench seat, although the comment had definitely been directed to Slocum in the rear of the wagon.

Slocum stirred and looked around at the pair. And what a pair they were.

Zeb Matthews was older than dirt and about the same color, burned to a dark nut brown from long hours traipsing around in the Mojave Desert most of his life before drifting north to Death Valley and finding work as a mule skinner. He claimed to have been with the original party of prospectors that had taken a wrong turn on the Old Spanish Trail and had blundered through this arid, burning hell of a land.

Only one man, an old geezer named Culverwell, who had been struck sick long before the wagons rolled across this particular desert, had died. Slocum believed Zeb on this part. What he didn't believe were the stories of how hot it had been. Slocum recollected the meandering prospectors had blundered through these parts in December, when it would have been colder than a witch's tit.

Zeb's partner, clutching his shotgun as if it might sprout wings and fly off if he relaxed, was years younger and could belch forth some of the wildest stories Slocum had ever heard, as if trying to keep up with his older partner.

Bennie Benson was a tad on the gullible side and solemnly assured everyone who would listen that at least a hundred men, women and children had died in that first expedition and that Zeb was only trying to put a good face on their deaths because he had chosen Death Valley as his home after getting his brains cooked.

There might be some truth to Zeb's stories, but he wasn't above having a little fun at the expense of his young friend. Slocum tried not to listen to them swapping increasingly improbable stories. It was too hot, too damned hot, and it was hardly eight o'clock.

The wagon hit a rock and almost threw Slocum out of the bed. He grabbed, caught himself on the splintery side and settled back down on a pile of smelly burlap bags he had tossed into the wagon to make the ride more comfortable. The idea was good, but the bags weren't enough padding by half. He preferred having a decent horse under him, but the owner of the Silver Emperor Mine, Big Pete Wilson, had refused to risk another animal in the stifling heat. Drivers, guards, miners, those didn't matter much to Wilson, but he took real good care of his horses and mules. Slocum reckoned the mine owner knew what was valuable in this furnace and what wasn't.

Mostly, the silver in the back of the wagon was prized above all else. Slocum idly pushed the tarpaulin back with one foot and caught sight of the crates holding the bright, shiny silver bars. The ore at the Silver Emperor in the Argus Mountains out near Wildrose Peak was incredibly rich in carbonates, and Wilson smelted it on the spot to reduce the weight transported out of Death Valley, through Towne

Pass to Panamint City on the other side of the mountains. From there even larger shipments from half a dozen mines made their way across Owens Lake on a boat and finally overland to San Francisco.

Just getting Wilson's silver to Panamint City had its upside and its downside. Upside meant every shipment carried a king's ransom.

The downside was why Benson rode shotgun and Slocum bounced around in the rear of the wagon, both men armed to the teeth. Such rich shipments drew road agents like flies to fresh cow flop. Slocum had worked for Wilson almost a month now and had ridden guard on two prior shipments. Both had been attacked. Asking others at the mine had revealed that there was seldom any shipment that wasn't set upon by the gang calling themselves the Mojave Guns.

Slocum didn't care what the outlaws called their gang or where they hailed from. They bled if they were shot, and that was all that mattered to him. That and not getting himself cut down protecting $7500 worth of silver.

Looking at the crate gave Slocum a pang, but it passed quickly. Often enough he had been on the other side of the law, riding with the road agents, bandanna pulled up over his nose to hide his identity, six-gun out and firing. The risk had been high but the rewards were higher, compared to riding along protecting the shipment for a measly thirty dollars a month, room and board. But Slocum was a man of his word and Wilson had given him a job when he needed it most. He had promised to get the silver shipments through safely, and so far he was doing a good job of it. The two prior shipments had arrived so the silver bars could be stashed in the Panamint City bank vault. This would be his third shipment. If those two yahoos in the driver's box didn't stop yammering incessantly, Slocum would make it his last.

"You ever felt heat like this, Slocum?" called Zeb. "Burns the hair right off your head, cooks your brains, then—"

Slocum sat bolt upright, then struggled to get to his knees in the bouncing wagon. He saw a small cloud of dust off to the left of the road, billowing up from a deep, dry ravine.

"What's that?" asked Benson, craning around to see what had spooked Slocum. "Might be a dust devil. Those whirlin' sons o' bitches can strip the flesh right off your bones. Don't seem possible, but I seen it with my own eyes, not a year back over at Mahogany Flat."

"Riders," Slocum said without elaborating. The only riders they were likely to encounter in the middle of Death Valley wanted to add to that name by leaving the lifeless bodies of drivers and guards to desiccate in the sun.

"They comin' after us?"

"You tell him, Zeb," Slocum said, grabbing his Winchester and levering a round into the chamber. The rising dust was still the only sign of the approaching riders, but it had betrayed them as surely as if they had come charging up with a full brass band blaring. Slocum didn't think much of their robbing technique since chasing down a heavily laden wagon, while not hard, was a damn sight more arduous than rolling a rock across the road, waiting for the driver to slow up, then springing an ambush. This way worked up a river of sweat that wasn't necessary.

"Old son," Zeb said, snapping the reins on the mules pulling the wagon to get them moving faster, "they ain't out here for their health. Fact is, they're out here to make sure we don't keep ours."

A bullet sailed through the air so far above their heads Slocum wondered why the outlaws had bothered. Might be they were green and a touch of buck fever had seized them. In Slocum's mind that made them even more dangerous. They'd fling lead around wildly and stood a better chance of hitting someone accidentally than if they were trying to fire accurately from horseback at a distance of a hundred yards.

"You get a shot at 'em, Slocum?" Zeb kept up his futile attempt to get more speed out of the balky mules. They pulled steadily and, in the desert heat, that was all that could be expected from them. He reached down and picked up his long blacksnake whip, gave it a flick to unroll it and then reared back and cracked it above the big-eared lead mule. They rolled along a little faster. But not much more. Not enough to outrun men on horses.

"I don't see 'em," Benson said, his voice turning shrill with fear. "All I see is that damned shimmery curtain o' heat out there." He let out a yelp, stood and unloaded with both barrels of his shotgun. The recoil knocked him backward, he caught his heel against the edge of the driver's box and tumbled to the ground.

"Danged fool," grumbled Zeb, having to pull back hard on the reins and stand to stomp his foot against the brake. Wood creaked as the bar grated against the front wheel, and they came to a halt. The driver looped the reins around the brake and jumped down to see why Benson wasn't moving.

"Get back here. Let him get his own worthless carcass into the wagon," Slocum complained. He stood, squared himself and aimed carefully at the rapidly approaching road agents. Slocum had been a sniper during the war and a good one. His shot was a little rushed but not enough to matter. He saw one outlaw's hat go flying through the air. Whether Slocum's bullet had set it sailing or if it had come off because of the man bending forward to get more speed out of his horse didn't matter. The outlaw veered and blundered into the path of his partner. The two horses collided and went down in a squealing, screaming pile. That left two other highwaymen.

Slocum's next shot went wide but caused the remaining pair to break off their attack. They circled warily, firing their six-shooters to no good effect because of the extreme range. Slocum didn't think much of this gang, if they were the Mojave Guns, because of the ineptness of their attack. That didn't mean they weren't dangerous.

Under the burning desert sun, anything out of the ordinary could be fatal.

"You about got him into the wagon?" Slocum shouted to Zeb.

"Ain't no need," the driver said. "Fool busted his neck

when he fell off the wagon." The driver climbed back into the wagon, laid Benson's shotgun down in the foot well and unfastened the reins from around the brake handle. Getting the mules pulling took a bit of skill and an active application of his long whip. The *snap*! of the whip convinced the mules to lurch against their harnesses and get the silver-laden wagon rolling once more.

"You kill any of them varmints? Explaining how we lost a guard's gonna be a chore, believe you me," Zeb said. His tanned face gleamed with sweat as he used his whip until the mules couldn't be urged to a faster gait. "But I'd rather 'splain Bennie's bein' dead than how we lost the silver."

"Brought down two of them, but nothing permanent," Slocum said, bracing himself as the wagon lurched around a bend in the road. He considered jumping down and ambushing the road agents as they came after the silver, but such a scheme might leave him stranded on foot in the desert. The road was well enough rutted that he could find his way back to the Silver Emperor Mine, but direction was less of a problem than being on foot without water. He wouldn't last an hour in the sun.

"Then we got problems 'cuz we can't outrun 'em," Zeb said. "Get Bennie's scattergun reloaded for me, and we'll see about gettin' 'em in a crossfire. Ain't no other way we're gonna convince them to let us be."

Slocum leaned over to grab the shotgun in the foot well when a sound like a cannon discharging rumbled up from beneath him. The wagon sagged, then bucked like a sunfishing bronco, throwing him clear. He hit the ground hard and managed to roll. He still accumulated skinned shoulders and arms as he slid across the alkali ground and fetched up hard against a rugged boulder next to the twin ruts that passed for a road. Painfully standing, he looked around for his rifle but it was nowhere to be found. Hand flashing to the ebony-handled Colt Navy in his cross-draw holster, he drew and fanned off three quick shots. Slocum was rewarded with a grunt, followed by silence.

"Got one of them," he shouted to Zeb. "You get that

shotgun loaded yet?" He didn't hear any movement from the direction of the wagon and nothing from the garrulous driver, but he wanted to give the remaining road agents the impression he and Zeb were ready and willing to fight to the death.

Continued silence, save for the braying mules, warned him that he might be the only one fighting to the death. It never occurred to him to offer the silver to the outlaws in exchange for his life. Such a crime meant a necktie party if Big Pete Wilson lost so much as an ounce of his precious silver.

For the outlaws, it was better not to leave witnesses. They might be greenhorns when it came to thieving, but Slocum wasn't going to make the mistake of thinking they were also stupid.

He edged back to the wagon and confirmed his suspicion of what had happened. The front axle had snapped as the wagon drove over a rock. The mules refused to stop their infernal braying, but this bothered Slocum less than the way Zeb Matthews lay on the ground, his arm bent around at an angle that meant he had broken it in his fall. That he wasn't moaning or thrashing about in pain worried Slocum even more. Dropping to one knee, he pressed his hand down on the driver's chest. The man's heart continued to beat somewhat weakly, enough to show that he was too tough to be killed as easily as Benson.

"Come on, old man, get up." Slocum shook Zeb, but he only moaned. The eyelids barely fluttered. Sounds on the far side of the road told Slocum he had more company, and they weren't likely to be friendly after he had drilled one of their partners.

Slocum got off a quick shot that did nothing but force the outlaw coming for him down into an arroyo. Fumbling around, keeping his eye on the terrain for any movement, Slocum retrieved the fallen shotgun, then went to the wagon. Benson had been careless about stashing the box of shells. When the axle broke, the shells had scattered all over the place. Slocum grabbed as many as he could without taking time to hunt, stuffed them into his coat pocket, then headed farther down the road, using the mules as cover for as long as he could. As he went, he loaded the shotgun and immediately used it.

The blast caught one outlaw in the leg and forced him down. Then there was only quiet. The mules stopped their caterwauling, the hot wind had died and Slocum was left with the sound of his own pulse roaring in his ears. A few quick breaths settled his nerves. He reloaded and went hunting for road agents.

Slocum wasn't sure if he was lucky or not. The trail of blood leading from the spot where he had hit the outlaw with the shotgun pellets told the tale. He and a partner had hightailed it. Slocum hadn't heard any pounding of hooves as the gang left, but he had been occupied with staying alive. Prowling around, he assured himself that they had left—but that didn't mean they wouldn't be back. The three men might fetch the rest of their gang since Slocum had heard the Mojave Guns numbered a dozen or more.

He stalked back to the wagon to find Zeb stirring weakly. The old galoot sat up, screeched like a barn owl and clutched at his arm.

"Dang it, busted the fool thing again," he said, looking up at Slocum. "That's three times in my goldurned life I've busted the same arm." Slocum said nothing, taking his time to be sure the old man's arm was securely tied down close to his body.

"You get them varmints? All of 'em?"

"Got one. The other three hightailed it," Slocum said.

"Well, git me back into the driver's box and we—" Zeb stared at Slocum. "The axle's broke, ain't it?"

"No way to fix it, 'less you brought along a spare," Slocum answered.

Zeb stood, took a few tottering footsteps, paused and then keeled over without making a sound. Slocum hurried to him, but the pain had been too much. Slocum dragged him into the dubious shade afforded by the crippled wagon, then dropped beside him on the hot ground to think. When the road agents reported their failure to their leader, even more would return. Slocum couldn't hope to sling all the silver on the backs of the mules and keep moving toward the pass over the Panamint Mountains, not with Zeb's arm the way it was and the driver unconscious. Repairing the wagon was out of the question.

Slocum saw only one way to save the silver and himself. Heaving to his feet, grumbling as he worked, he stripped back the dusty tarp and heaved one crate of silver after another out of the wagon until all five of the hundred pound crates were out. It took him the better part of an hour, using the reluctant mules, to carry the silver some distance from the road into a particularly rugged section of rocks and bury it. After he finished his chore, he stepped back and studied the spot critically. If any searcher stood more than a few feet away, it looked like every other stretch of the godforsaken land. There wasn't a hint that the earth had been dug and replaced, much less that a young fortune in silver lay just beneath the surface.

Getting his bearings, Slocum returned to the wagon, stripped it of what remained of their water supply—four desert bags of tepid water—and heaved Zeb over the back of the lead mule. Working carefully, it took ten minutes for Slocum to lash the driver into place so he wouldn't fall off, but he was eventually satisfied with his diamond hitch and the way the old man rode, belly-down. He rubbed his hindquarters in anticipation and then climbed onto another mule. Slocum preferred a speedier horse under him, but anything with four legs was better than walking through Death Valley on his own boot leather.

Leading the other protesting mules, Clint kept Zeb's close by so he could watch the driver's condition as they rode. He cut due east off the road and then returned to the Silver Emperor Mine by a circuitous route designed to keep the outlaws off his trail.

It was nigh on sundown when he spotted the lights at the mine. Slocum wasn't sure if facing the outlaws—and the desert—wasn't preferable to telling Big Pete Wilson what had happened.

2

The mules brayed loudly and brought a drove of off-shift miners pouring out of the bunkhouses. In the distance, Slocum saw the dark open mouth of the main tunnel of the Silver Emperor Mine. A solitary lantern swung in front of it to mark where the night watchman stood. Big Pete Wilson had learned the hard way about high-graders sneaking into his claim at night, taking the best nuggets they could, even doing some mining on the lead carbonate veins to get some good quality ore and slipping away before the morning shift showed up for work. The loss of the ore had irked him mightily, but Slocum thought the high-graders using Wilson's own equipment had rankled even more. All they had to do was load the ore on their own pack animals and get away.

They might even have stolen the mules and horses.

"That you, Slocum?"

"None other," Slocum said, swinging down off the mule he had ridden all day long. "Can you and some of the boys get the animals watered and fed? And Zeb's all banged up. He needs some attention right away."

"Doc's asleep by now. Been a tough day fer us, Slocum. There was a cave-in down on the south stope. Doc's spent the better part of the day patchin' up some folks, buryin' others." The miner cast a fearful glance downslope toward

10

the small cemetery that had almost doubled in size since Slocum had ridden out that morning.

"Zeb's going to be planted down there with them if he doesn't get some attention," Slocum said. "Arm's busted."

"Again? I do declare, that man's got cooked chicken bones 'stead of real ones in his arm. His right arm, too, I bet?"

Slocum nodded agreement, and this produced a belly laugh.

"That old coot ain't gonna be dealin' off the bottom of no deck fer a spell." The miner began unlashing Zeb from the mule, almost cooing like a pigeon as he worked. Slocum hadn't heard more than a groan or two from the driver all day long, even when he spilled water into his parched mouth, but the miner provoked Zeb enough to elicit a string of profanity. Slocum had to admit this might have been what Zeb needed to goad him back to his senses.

There hadn't been much Slocum could do in the way of conversation, not going through all four of their water bags before the sun had reached its hottest past midday.

"Where's the damned wagon?"

"Good to see you, Mr. Wilson. Pleasant evening," Slocum said. He took off his hat and beat it against his leg, causing a miniature dust storm to rise. The mine owner coughed and futilely tried to shoo it away.

"Where's the damned silver?"

"Bennie Benson got killed," Slocum said in a level tone. He knew the man's interests were more in the hardware and the shipment than with the men guarding and transporting it, but Slocum was feeling downright ornery riding a mule all day under the burning hot sun after being shot at.

"You brung back all the animals?"

"All of them, including Zeb Matthews," Slocum said. "He broke his arm again and was unconscious most of the day."

Wilson planted himself squarely in front of Slocum, having to look up into cold green eyes from a height of only five-nine or thereabouts. Slocum had a good three inches on the man and more than thirty pounds, all of it rawhide and whipcord muscle. Wilson had a fleshy look to him from being hidden from the sun most of the day, but Slocum had a tad of respect for the man. He was a decent mining engineer and, for all his avarice, he had never risked a miner's life underground. Aboveground was a different concern, and one Slocum intended to address.

"Did Benson have any family? You ought to let them know he died defending your silver shipment."

"Was it the Mojave Guns?" Wilson's face clouded with anger. He turned and spat and only then did he face Slocum again, his chin thrust upward belligerently. "It was them varmints," he said positively. "I know it was them! I'm gonna put a reward on their heads so big every bounty hunter in Nevada and California'll come flockin' here to collect!"

Wilson stormed about, waving his arms, ranting and raving and finally cooled down enough to come back and glare at Slocum again.

"Where's the damned silver? Did they take the silver?"

Slocum understood the question that was meant rather than the one Wilson asked. He wanted to know why Slocum and Zeb were still alive if the Mojave Guns had attacked. They had been hired to get the silver shipment to Panamint City and hadn't died. That made them accomplices, in his eyes.

"The outlaws didn't get it," Slocum said. Wilson started to berate him further, then he stopped, mouth open like a fish washed up on a muddy shore.

"Where's it? Not on them mules. They walked in here without any load but you and Zeb."

"That's right," Slocum said, enjoying his little torment of the mine owner. When he imagined steam coming out the man's ears, he went on in his slow Southern drawl. "The wagon broke an axle, Benson was dead, Zeb was laid up, so I did what I had to do."

"What was that?" Big Pete Wilson looked suspicious now. "You didn't barter your worthless hides for it, did you?"

"Wouldn't have worked," Slocum said. "They would have killed us if I'd tried."

"Damned right, they would have. Where's the silver?"

"Buried. I dragged it a hundred yards away from the wagon and buried it so we can take another wagon down in the morning and fetch it. Or take it on into Panamint City, if you have a decent driver. That's a mighty rough road for someone who doesn't know how to handle a mule team."

"You buried it? What if they saw you?"

"They didn't. They would have come hootin' and hollerin' and shootin'," Slocum said. "No reason they'd want to go to the trouble of digging it up so's I wouldn't know about it."

"The whole shipment? Every single ounce of silver? Buried? And you know where it is?"

"That's right," Slocum said. His belly rumbled from lack of food and his mouth felt like the inside of a cotton bale. Nothing sounded finer to him right at the moment than some chow, all the water he could guzzle and a night between the blankets.

"I'll round up a few of the miners, and we kin go watch over the silver until a wagon shows up," Wilson said.

Slocum stared at the man. His cold green eyes locked with Wilson's muddy brown ones.

"I'm too tuckered out to find the spot. Might be easier if we went in the morning."

"But it's out there. Unguarded!"

"You got the whole of Death Valley to protect your silver overnight," Slocum said. "Anybody who finds the silver and makes off with it just might deserve it. But that's not going to happen. See that Zeb's taken care of properlike, and I'm going to get some victuals."

Slocum left Wilson sputtering as he walked toward the mess hall set between two barracks where the miners slept. The fragrance of stew still drifted from the mess hall, making his mouth water. That alone was worth the walk to the building, feeling moisture in his mouth again. Slocum got himself the leftover stew, a hunk of dry bread and what must have been a gallon of water and set about to eating.

One by one the men came by to hear his story, but he put them off, saying that Zeb would do it justice. Only when Doc Lonigan came in did Slocum slow the pace of his eating and drinking to belch, lean back and ask, "How's Zeb getting on?"

"He's too tough to die. You shoulda rode him back and saved the mule," Lonigan said. The man wasn't actually a doctor and had told Wilson that straight out when he'd been hired, but he had worked as a doctor's aide during the war and had become proficient enough patching minor injuries that he had moved from miner to medic at the same pay, spending time sorting ore when his medical abilities weren't required.

"He said his arm'd been broke before. I've seen men lose their arms and legs when that happens too many times."

"Not this time," Lonigan said, pouring himself a tin cup of water and downing it in a single draft. Not many men could get enough to drink working in a mine in the middle of Death Valley, and Lonigan was in their ranks.

"Glad to hear it. I asked Wilson if he knew of any family Benson might have—"

"None. He was just a drifter. Don't rightly know what to do. We could leave him for the buzzards but that don't seem right. Don't seem right throwin' him into the wagon and takin' him on into Panamint City, either. And gettin' him back here to our own boneyard's not too likely."

"Could leave him when we go on to Panamint City," Slocum said, thinking about it, "then pick him up on the way back? That gets the silver to the bank without a jinx on it and Benson can get buried all properlike."

"All we need's a wagon." Lonigan grinned. "Reckon you know where we'll get it, too?"

"The charcoal wagon? It's due soon?"

"In the morning, all the way from the kilns over in Wildrose Canyon." Lonigan grinned even more broadly.

"Don't reckon you'd want anyone else but you doin' the dickerin' to borrow that wagon, either."

Slocum snorted and went back to his meal, but he was glad things had worked out this way. The heavy wagon delivered charcoal three times a week for the smelter a ways down the canyon—and its driver was about the best looking woman this side of the Rockies. Mira Nell Van Winkle had taken a fancy to Slocum, and it had been mutual. The past month had been filled with deadly days guarding the silver shipments, but the nights had been equally as exciting riding and breaking that pretty filly.

"Better get some sleep, Slocum," Lonigan said. "Wilson will want you to set out the minute the charcoal wagon's unloaded."

"Thanks, Doc. Go look after Zeb. Tell him I'll stand his shift this time."

"I do that and I'll never hear the end of it." Doc Lonigan left whistling tunelessly through the gap in his lower teeth.

Slocum perched on the rock beside the road, looking more like a lean, hungry vulture than a suitor. The sun was barely rising above the mountains to his back when he heard the clatter of chains and the creaking of wood and leather bridle as the wagon lumbered up the road from the Modock Consolidated Mining Company owned by George Hearst. He and Wilson had been partners for a spell before each had struck it big. Hearst had found a rich vein of silver to the west in the Argus Mountains and Wilson had discovered the Silver Emperor. They had reached an agreement between them that Hearst would own the kilns but Wilson could purchase all the charcoal he needed for his own smelting. Slocum had seldom seen such an arrangement work long before one partner got a bit greedy and tried to do the other out of his share, but everyone said Hearst and Wilson remained good friends.

He didn't much care if they spat at each other like angry cats as long as Mira Van Winkle had her perky behind planted on the driver's seat and brought the wagon up this road so he could talk to her again. He caught sight of the sun glinting off her raven-dark hair as it flowed back on a hot morning breeze. She had her hat slung down, dangling from its cord around her neck to let the air flow past her finely boned oval face. But it was her bow-shaped lips that Slocum found himself admiring most. Or was it the ample flare of her womanly hips? Or could it be the surge of her firm breasts under the man's denim work shirt she had tailored to fit her every curve? Or the way both their bodies seemed to fit together perfectly as they lay side by side? Slocum decided everything about her body was just fine, but he appreciated more than this. She was as witty and capable as anyone he had ever come across.

"John!" she called, waving. "I thought you were going to Panamint City with a shipment. How good to see you back so soon!"

As she drove the heavily laden wagon past, Slocum stepped off the rock and settled beside her on the bench seat. Their legs pressed together warmly. Somehow the heat didn't bother either of them.

"Ran into a bit of trouble." He explained Wilson's need for the wagon by the time they reached the smelter.

"I don't see why Mr. Hearst would mind. Besides, he's in San Francisco on business and Pa's in charge."

Mira's father worked as superintendent of the kilns but otherwise might have had to ask permission to loan the wagon since it was the only one Modock Consolidated used to freight the charcoal.

"I'm sure Wilson can afford to rent the wagon, if there'd be any loss from delayed charcoal shipments," Slocum said.

"That's true, but I think there might be more payment than that required," Mira said, looking coquettishly out of the corner of her eye and smiling.

"What extra payment might that be?" Slocum asked, enjoying the game.

"We'd have to negotiate, you and me. Might take a while."

"All night, I reckon."

"Promises, promises!" she laughed. Mira waved to the men from Wilson's smelter to begin unloading the shipment. The black dust rising as they shoveled out the back of the wagon left them coughing and filthy, but none complained in the woman's hearing. Slocum knew they swore sulfurously when they thought she wasn't listening. Mira had good ears and was amused by their manners.

"All done. You takin' the wagon now, Slocum?" called the smelter foreman.

Slocum glanced at Mira, then said, "I'll take Miss Van Winkle to the mine. She can keep Zeb company 'til we get back."

"I'll ride that far with you," she said as Slocum snapped the reins and got the team pulling. They'd need at least four more mules for the wagon after they retrieved the silver, more than Mira was able to control. Even so, Slocum wondered if she wouldn't do a better job driving than he would. Mules were different critters from horses and had minds of their own.

Just like Mira.

"I'll look in on Zeb. Doc Lonigan can keep that old fool company. I don't need to. I'll sneak a bite to eat and get a horse to ride back to the kilns. You can drive the wagon over when you get back, then ride the horse back to the Silver Emperor."

"You've got it all worked out," Slocum said. Mira never stopped thinking. That was just one of the things about her that attracted him. Others were bouncing about as they hit one rock in the road after another.

"You're deliberating taking the roughest part of the road," she accused.

"View's not bad."

She poked him in the ribs with an elbow, and they joshed one another until they came within sight of the mine. Mira settled down then and was almost sedate by the time Big Pete Wilson helped her down.

"Pleased to see you Miss Mira," he said. "And you men, get the supplies loaded. Hitch up two more pair of mules. You'll have a lot more weight to pull soon enough." Wilson hesitated. "I ought to go with you, just to be sure."

"The silver'll be delivered to Panamint City," Slocum said. "You've got my promise."

"It'd better. I've got to cover a big purchase of new equipment and supplies."

"I'm sure Mr. Slocum will help cover . . . things," Mira said impishly. She batted her long dark eyelashes at him, then grinned wickedly. If he could have grown wings and flown to the silver, he would have.

"Stop lollygagging and get on the road, Slocum," Wilson ordered.

Slocum glanced over his shoulder and saw the four men in the wagon had settled down. They were already filthy with the charcoal left from the shipment to the smelter. Slocum gee-hawed and got the mules pulling, driving them faster with the empty wagon. The four behind him chattered like old women, nervously looking around for the outlaws. Soon enough, Slocum reached the broke-down wagon, drew rein and jumped to the ground.

"This the spot, Slocum?" One miner looked apprehensive.

"You saw Benson's body back along the road, didn't you?" asked Slocum. The man nodded numbly. Slocum knew he had to reassure the men or find himself with a mutiny on his hands—or worse. Any of the miners might get buck fever and start shooting. Slocum didn't want them sitting behind him in the wagon if they didn't know exactly what they were aiming at.

"Those road agents are long gone. If they thought the silver was around here, they'd have hunted for a while and given up."

Slocum led the way, the four trailing him like ducklings behind their mother, all the way to the spot where he had hidden the crates. For a fearful moment, Slocum failed to identify the right spot and then he worried the outlaws had actually found the stash. Then he kicked away a pile of stones and saw a wood lid where he had left it.

"Get to it," Slocum said, relieved. It took them as long to wrestle the crates back to the wagon as it had taken him to use the mules and then bury the silver. He made sure the crates were secured properly in the rear of the wagon, stood in the box and squinted at the heat-hazy horizon. All he saw along this stretch of Death Valley road belonged here.

He dropped to the hard bench and coaxed the mules to begin pulling with a full load. His shoulders ached and he was in dire need of a few shots of whiskey by the time they arrived in Panamint City, but they did arrive just past midnight. He had to drag the bank president out of bed to open the vault to store the silver, but the man didn't seem too upset when he saw how much there was.

Slocum heaved a sigh of relief when he accepted the receipt for the 450 pounds of precious metal. He thanked the bank officer, then had a few drinks in the wide-open boomtown's most raucous saloon just to wet his whistle. Finally, he went to the stables, found a nice pile of straw in the stall next to a striking palomino and fell into a deep sleep, dreaming of silver and Mira Nell Van Winkle.

3

Slocum drove the charcoal wagon down the road smack in the center of Wildrose Canyon, wishing the mules would pull faster. The guards with him slept noisily in the rear, feeling the effects of too much Panamint City whiskey. All Slocum could think of was Mira waiting for him at the charcoal kilns. He smiled broadly when he saw her curvy trim figure move out from behind the end kiln and wave. He waved back, snapped the reins to keep the mules pulling and found they had developed minds of their own.

The mules smelled water pouring into a huge pond a ways off and wanted to drink until they had their fill. Slocum knew the mules weren't as likely as a horse to drink until they bloated, but he wanted to be sure. The cool, sweet water burbling up from the ground was mighty tempting, even to a man who knew better than to drink too much too fast.

"Let them go," Mira urged. "The boys'll watch them."

"I've got four more in the back of the wagon you can have," Slocum said. "I hadn't figured on them so they'll either have to walk or stay here until Wilson can send horses for them."

"I remembered," Mira said haughtily. "When I rode your horse over, I brought four more. They're in the corral down by the main office. But your big trouble's going to be

20

keeping those fellows in the saddle. Not a one of 'em looks sober."

"We buried Bennie Benson out on the road instead of hauling his corpse back. Seemed the thing to do. That's why they finished the quart bottle of rotgut they'd bought in Panamint City so fast."

Slocum pulled the wagon around and judged distances. He released the mules to drink their fill, then silently motioned to Mira to help him. Together they rolled the wagon backward toward the pond. He opened the rear gate and began rolling the men out one by one. The first hadn't stopped yelling in surprise, sitting waist deep in the water, before the fourth one was splashing about. Their empty whiskey bottle rolled after them, splashed into the water and bobbed about.

"Cool off, then we'll ride on back to the mine," Slocum told them. "Horses are in the corral yonder." The foursome growled and grumbled and then began enjoying their impromptu swim. Slocum knew they'd be at it for some time, giving him the chance to talk with Mira. He wished he had time for more than exchanging a few words.

"You're about the prettiest sight in all of Death Valley," he told her.

She smiled, then sobered. Mira pushed some of her black hair from her sky-bright blue eyes and looked squarely at him. "I've got some bad news."

"What?"

"Zeb died."

"How'd that happen?" Slocum was startled at the news. He hadn't thought the old-timer would ever die, not after surviving an entire day of riding belly-down over a mule and with a broken arm.

"Doc Lonigan said he took a fever sometime in the night. Came on fast. He was so weakened that he just gave up the ghost."

Slocum hadn't known Zeb Matthews all that well, but he had liked him as much as anyone in the Silver Emperor Mine camp.

"Reckon I ought to get back. Funeral'll be today."

"Might already have him in the ground. Doc Lonigan said the infection had spread fast, and he didn't want to risk anybody else getting a touch of it."

"Seen that during the war," Slocum said. One man got gangrene and another, usually with an open wound, brushed against the infection, transferring it. It was best if Zeb found his eternal resting place quickly.

"You've seen a lot, haven't you?" Mira looked down at the worn handle of his Colt Navy slung low on his left hip. She'd never seen him draw, but the cross-draw holster was slung like a gunfighter's.

"Not a bit of it matches seeing more of you," he said, lightening the mood.

"Oh, you," Mira said, hitting him hard in the chest. Slocum flinched from the hard, strong fist, then grabbed her and pulled Mira close to give her a quick kiss. "Oh, *you*!" she repeated but with more feeling. The woman sagged a little in his arms.

"Later," he told her. "I'll bet a month's pay Wilson already has enough chores thought up for me to keep an army busy. He's not one to let the moss grow under any of his paid workmen."

"I wouldn't mind feeling a little moss under me," Mira said in a dreamy voice. "Under my naked body, with your naked—" She jerked back, eyes going wide when the four men sloshed from the pond and lumbered toward them.

"You 'bout ready to ride, Slocum?" asked the shortest of the lot. "We're willin' to stay here till hell freezes over, but Mr. Wilson he gets kinda antsy when his men don't git on back to camp accordin' to schedule."

"Let's ride," Slocum ordered. The five walked down the road to the Modock Consolidated corral, found their gear, saddled and rode out within ten minutes. It took the better part of an hour to negotiate the trail through Wildrose Canyon and up toward Emigrant Pass and the Silver Emperor Mine. As they rode into camp they passed the small cemetery. Slocum saw the new grave without a marker and knew it had to be Zeb's. He'd see to putting a stone or wood cross on it when he could.

"Slocum!" came the loud shout from the direction of the mine. Big Pete Wilson came hurrying downslope, waving his arms like a windmill without a governor. "Get on over here. I need to talk to you."

Slocum dismounted and walked to where the mine owner fumed and fussed.

"I forgot to tell you to pick up supplies in town. Plumb slipped my mind. You got to go back and get things, including a new axle to fix the wagon out there on the road. I could have some of the boys from the mine fashion one, but it's better to let a wheelwright do it since 'bout all we got is green wood, and that's no good for an axle."

Wilson had developed quite a case of verbal diarrhea and Slocum knew why. The more he talked, the less he had to say about Zeb's death. Realizing the man's reason for the continuous flow of orders, Slocum said nothing and took it all in.

"You can sign against the silver put into that bank. You have the receipt? Good," Wilson said, taking it without so much as a glance and stuffing it into a pocket already bulging with other papers. "Things have begun to jump around here. We found a new vein. Bigger 'n better than the one we followed down in the first place. Stand to make a fortune on it. Got all manner of deals ridin' on it bein' the biggest and best."

"I'll need a paper telling the bank president I'm allowed to buy against your account."

"Got that all done up, legal and proper," Wilson said, handing it over.

Slocum glanced at it, hesitated, then read it carefully. He looked up at Wilson.

"This says I'm your foreman."

"You got promoted. Been considerin' how you hid the silver and all. Good thinkin', you saved a big shipment. Might have saved the mine, especially now that we need a whale of a lot more equipment to work the new silver vein. Blue dirt! You can't believe the carbonate in there. Or maybe you can. You know something about minin'. I can always tell."

Slocum had done his share of hard-rock mining and had learned to hate it. Being underground all day cut off his horizons. Breathing rock dust and living by the guttering light of miners' candles was no fit way to spend a life, and the dangers there were more out of control than aboveground. He could shoot it out with an outlaw but if a timber gave way, there was no amount of arguing that would convince a cave-in to move.

"The wagon's back at the charcoal kilns," he said. Slocum wouldn't mind a return to Wildrose Canyon and Mira Van Winkle. Considering the time of day, he would arrive around twilight and have to spend the night. That would be a fine way of celebrating his promotion to mine foreman.

"Take pack mules. Four will do. You can figure how to sling an axle so we can repair our wagon. The rest of the supplies, well, here's the list. Lots of dynamite. Blasting caps, black fuse, supplies."

"Four cases of champagne?" Slocum saw Wilson's face break into a smile.

"Reckon everybody ought to do a little celebratin' 'bout the new vein of ore."

"Dynamite and champagne," Slocum said, shaking his head. It was as explosive a mixture as he had ever hauled.

"You handle it by yourself? I need to get as many picks workin' on that ore as quick as I can. I'm anxious to find what's really there."

"Count on me," Slocum said. "You want me to leave right away or can I grab some grub?"

The question obviously forced Big Pete Wilson to make a decision he wanted to avoid. He heaved a sigh and finally said, "Eat. Get your horse ready, pick the mules, but you clear out as quick as you can so you can get back here. Understand?"

"I do. Thanks for the promotion." Slocum thrust out his

hand. Wilson shook it hard, his soft hand grating against Slocum's callused one.

Slocum was back on the trail to Panamint City within the hour.

Slocum rode slowly into Panamint City, the six mules trailing behind doggedly. He had been in town so many times in the past few days he wondered if the mayor ought to give him the keys to the city. It was hours till dawn but most of the saloons were still roaring. Bad piano playing was the first thing Slocum noticed as he rode past many of them, but the fights and general carousing were universal. He got the mules to the livery stables and penned them in the corral, making sure they had feed and enough water. From the look of the horses in the corral, their owners had neglected them something fierce.

"Probably too drunk to remember to feed their own horses," Slocum muttered, wiping his dirty sleeve across his mouth. He was dog-tired after riding miles through burning sun and then even more miles after the temperature had dropped to the point where the tip of his nose was damned near frozen. But his mouth was sticky and dry, giving him ample excuse to knock back a whiskey or two before turning in for a few hours' sleep. There'd be plenty of time when the mining supply store opened in the morning to get Wilson's dynamite and other blasting supplies. Dickering with the wheelwright to get a new axle might take longer.

If Slocum had any kind of luck, he might be in town an extra day waiting on the axle.

As he walked toward the nearest saloon, his thoughts drifted back through Death Valley to Wildrose Canyon and the charcoal kilns with their lovely attendant. Slocum had never learned how Mira's father had come to be foreman of the kilns or why she was so good at business and about everything else. That was something he wanted to explore further, and loitering in Panamint City took away from his time doing it.

He could get the wheelwright to knock out a suitable axle by midday and be back at the Silver Emperor about this time the following night. Slocum preferred traveling through the desert at night, although the dark of the moon slowed his pace, because dealing with the cold was easier for him than the mind-numbing heat of the day.

He pushed through the doors of the saloon and saw that miners filled the large room shoulder to shoulder. Slocum almost backed away to find a less crowded gin mill but when he saw a small corner at the bar, he decided to go in. He pushed past a dozen rowdy miners and found the spot where he could put his back to the wall and comfortably watch the goings-on throughout the room. Unlike most saloons, this one didn't cater to the gamblers or even the lonely men searching for female companionship. The primary function of the place was simple: keep pouring the whiskey and drawing the beer until the customers fell over in a stupor. A piano player at the rear banged out tunes Slocum couldn't quite recognize, but this lack didn't matter to any of the other patrons.

They sang, some of them even singing the same song, loudly and with gusto.

"What'll it be?" asked the barkeep.

"Beer. Make it two. That way you don't have to come back."

"In a hurry to get drunk? We got a special tonight. Half bottle of tarantula juice for fifty cents. Guarantee that'll take you where you want to go. You'll be barkin' at the moon 'fore you know it."

"Two beers," Slocum repeated. The barkeep shrugged and went to draw them, bringing both back. He snared the two bits Slocum dropped on the counter and sent a nickle change spinning back.

Slocum sipped at the first beer and found it decently smooth. Too many saloons served bitter brew suited more for removing tar than for drinking.

Before he had drained half the beer, a ruckus started over by the entrance. Slocum turned to see three miners giving an Indian a hard time, pushing him from one side to the other. He finished the first beer, picked up the second and sampled it, then walked to the door.

"You gents about done funnin' with my friend?"

"Friend? This red nigger's yer friend?"

Slocum handed his beer to one of the miners and said, "Here, hold this for me." The instant the miner had the beer in his hand, Slocum reared back and unloaded a haymaker that landed in the speaker's belly. The man folded over, the air driven out of his lungs. Slocum spun, cut loose with three quick jabs that knocked the second miner to the floor, stunning him. He took the beer from the third man's hands and glared at him. The miner gulped and backed away.

"Come on," Slocum said to the Indian. "Unless you have a hankering to get kicked to death." They went into the cold night air. The muzziness Slocum had felt from drinking the first beer vanished as a breeze whipped down Panamint City's main street. He handed the beer to the Indian. "Drink up. I've lost my taste."

"You get in heap big trouble," the Indian said, staring at the frothy beer.

"So'll you if you get drunk. So don't get drunk."

The Indian downed the beer in a long, appreciative draft, then tossed the mug over his shoulder to rattle against the side of the saloon.

"You good man."

"What tribe?" asked Slocum.

"Timbisha."

"Oh, Shoshone." Slocum had heard about the Shoshones living in the center of Death Valley. They had to be tough to survive in such barren, forbidding land. The man in front of him was short, hardly five-foot-five but he was strongly muscled. Slocum had never been able to guess any Indian's age, but this one was around twenty and full of piss and vinegar.

"You looking for a job?"

"You give Burning Tree money?"

"If you work for it."

The Shoshone considered the matter for a few seconds, then nodded once, crossed his arms over his powerful chest and stared at Slocum.

"Three dollars," Slocum said, "if you help me load my mules and get the cargo back to the Silver Emperor Mine."

"Mine owned by Big Pete," Burning Tree said. He spat. "He no good to me, to Timbisha. Chase us off, beat with whips."

"Might be he's more inclined to treat you well now," Slocum said, thinking of Wilson's buoyant mood at finding a spectacular new silver vein.

"You promise money?"

"My name's Slocum and I promise." Slocum thrust out his hand. Burning Tree hesitated then grabbed it in a bone-crushing handshake to seal their deal.

"You give more beer? Firewater?"

"Don't press your luck," Slocum said, motioning the Indian to follow him to the stables. His long ride had caught up with him, and he needed to get a few hours of sleep. Barely had he dropped into the straw, his blanket wrapped around him than he came awake with a start, hand going to his six-shooter. It took him a second to realize the dark figure squatting at his feet belonged there. Burning Tree patiently waited for him to wake up.

He sneezed, wiped his nose and then squinted at the sun trying to snake through the chinks in the livery wall. It was already morning.

"Come on," Slocum said. "I need to talk to someone who can sell me dynamite and some champagne." He saw he had Burning Tree's undivided attention. "Don't you go getting ideas about touching any of it, dynamite or champagne."

Burning Tree solemnly shook his head.

Slocum stretched, stood, strapped on his gun belt and settled his six-gun. It was time to get to work. Burning Tree trailed him as he went to the mining supply store and got the explosives, then let the Indian strap the load onto a trio of mules.

"I've got to get the champagne. Can you talk to the wheelwright about an axle for a wagon?"

Burning Tree stood for a moment, staring blankly at him. "Well?"

"Me go? Me get axle for you?"

"That's why you're making the big money," Slocum said. Burning Tree smiled slowly, then nodded once. "If the wheelwright gives you any guff, tell him Mr. Wilson will take his business somewhere else, then wait for me." Again Burning Tree nodded once. "Go on. We have work to do."

The Shoshone walked off, head high. Slocum turned to the row of saloons, now quiet, and took better than twenty minutes before he found one that had four full cases of champagne that didn't look as if the bottles had been filled by the local barkeep. It might not be Grand Monopole but it would do to get the miners greased and let them know their boss appreciated their work—and the new silver strike.

Slocum loaded the champagne onto the fourth mule and went to find Burning Tree. To his surprise the Shoshone had negotiated a decent price and the wheelwright was finishing off the last of the burrs on the axle. Slocum paid, he and Burning Tree hefted the heavy wood rod and got it loaded onto the fifth mule. Slocum pointed to the sixth, silently indicating that Burning Tree had a ride back to the Silver Emperor.

The Shoshone climbed on and rode alongside the mule with the axle, as if he accepted the transportation of the axle as his special chore. This suited Slocum fine as he rode on his horse. It was a little after eleven. He could reach the mine before sundown, no matter how hot the sun might be, and he had the advantage of Burning Tree's presence. Any road agents spotting them would think twice about attacking two men where they might easily swoop down on a solitary freighter.

The trip to the mine was uneventful but riding into camp was anything but.

"You get outta here, you damn redskin!" shouted Wilson, arms flailing around when he spotted Burning Tree. "You tryin' to steal from us again? I'll horsewhip you!" Wilson reached for a crowbar and stopped dead when he heard the distinctive metallic sound of a six-shooter hammer cocking.

He looked up into the muzzle of Slocum's Colt Navy. It might have been .36 caliber but it had to look like the gaping mouth of a mine.

"Touch that and you're a dead man," Slocum said coldly.

4

"If you don't drop that crowbar, I'll drill you," Slocum said. His tone told the story. He wasn't joking.

"Damned thief! How'd he get my mule?" Big Pete Wilson had frozen, fingers around the iron rod, but he made no move to lift it or try to fling it at the Shoshone.

"I hired him to help with the supplies," Slocum said.

"You're fired!"

Slocum stared down at Wilson and saw how his face had flushed. The man had spittle flecking his lips and his hands shook.

"Ore peter out already?" Slocum asked.

"What?" The question took Wilson by surprise. "No, it's richer 'n I thought."

"Good luck," Slocum said. To Burning Tree Slocum called out, "Don't worry none about him." Slocum fumbled in his pocket and pulled out three silver dollars, passed them to the Shoshone and said, "You'd better go."

Burning Tree turned blank eyes on Slocum, nodded once, hit the ground and ran from the camp with an easy, long stride that devoured the distance and took him away quickly.

"There's the dynamite, the champagne, some supplies and your axle," Slocum said, using the six-shooter to point out the supplies brought in. With a flourish, he holstered his pistol and turned his horse's face to follow Burning Tree from the camp.

"Hold your horses, Slocum. Don't go off like that. I didn't mean nuthin'. You're not fired. I need you to help out. We got more work 'n you can shake a stick at."

Slocum stared back at the mine owner. Thoughts tumbled over and over like the wheels of that slot machine gambling gadget he had seen in San Francisco a while back. He had no idea what had set off Wilson, but it was ugly.

"Please." The word obviously burned Wilson's tongue.

"All right," Slocum said, "but you got some explaining to do."

This almost set off a new rage, but Wilson settled down and nodded curtly, about like Burning Tree had. The difference between the men lay in their eyes. Burning Tree's had been flat and emotionless. Wilson's still had a deadly fire blazing in them. Slocum dismounted and waited for the mine owner's explanation.

"We had all manner of thefts around here. Reckon it was Indians sneakin' in and robbin' us."

"You don't know that it was Burning Tree."

"That the cayuse's name?"

"I don't hear you saying why you acted the way you did."

"Never took you to be an Injun lover," Wilson said, turning surly.

"Can't say that I am, but then again, I don't cotton much to any man 'less he proves himself. Burning Tree worked for me, did what I told him, and didn't raise any fuss. *You* raised a fuss."

"They killed my family," Wilson blurted.

"The Shoshone?"

"Not them, not the ones livin' near here. The Crow, up north. They killed my wife and one on the way. We were hopin' for a boy, but I never found out." Wilson's hand began to shake again, but the fire in his eyes changed and gave him a distant stare, one seeing a place long ago and far away. "I can't abide them redskins, not after what they did to Claire and my unborn kid."

"Burning Tree wasn't the one, and from what you say, it wasn't any of his Shoshone tribe, either. They don't get along that well with the Crow."

"They're all the same," Wilson said in a grating voice. His hands balled into fists and he shook all over. "No Indians in this camp."

"All right, if that's the way you want it," Slocum said, "but I'm not going out of my way to make enemies with them. I know other tribes have done terrible things, but unless Burning Tree's does something to rile me, I'm not going to do anything against them."

"I got plenty of hate to go around," Wilson said. Slocum saw the red had faded from his face and the mine owner's hands unclenched. A little. He took a deep breath and said again, "Don't go, Slocum. You caught me at a bad time."

"I'm staying, for the time being," Slocum said, wondering if he wasn't letting another part of his body dictate to his good sense. If he rode out of the Silver Emperor camp, he might as well keep on riding since there wasn't another job to be had for a hundred miles. That meant he wasn't likely to see Mira Van Winkle again.

"Get that champagne up to the mess hall," Wilson called to a pair of miners working to unload the supplies. "Put it on ice, if we got any."

They grinned broadly and did as they were told. Wilson stood with his hands on his hips, staring at the axle still slung on the other mule.

"We need that wagon real bad, Slocum. You and one of the fellas who can fix things take it and get the wagon rolling again."

"Might be you could use a second wagon," Slocum said.

"Costs too much. Even with the new silver, it's too expensive and I'm pushed to the limit buyin' . . . things. We can make do, patchin' up the old one. Take Luther. I think he can fix 'bout anything and nuthin's busted in the mine right now. Even if it was, we need the wagon more." Wilson looked squarely at Slocum as if there was something more he wanted to say. The mine owner spun and stalked off.

Word spread through the camp like wildfire that they had four cases of champagne to pass around. Slocum waited for Luther to have a cup or two, and he even tasted it himself. It wasn't as bad as he had feared, but it was far from being the French champagne it was said to be on the label.

"The boss wants us to fix up the wagon," Slocum told Luther, a hulking, dour man with a pointed head and hands the size of quart jars. Slocum hadn't heard the man utter more than a dozen words in the past month. If he had been able to choose a partner to fix the wagon, he would have picked Burning Tree over Luther. But he only worked there.

"Got tole that already," Luther said, his words guttural and rumbling from deep in his barrel chest.

"Get what tools you'll need and sling them on a pack mule. You can ride another, then we can hitch them to the wagon and let them pull it back," Slocum said. Two mules ought to be strong enough to move the empty wagon, if the axle worked properly. Luther ambled off to get the tools while Slocum watered the mules, fed them and got them ready for the trip back into the hot desert.

He and Luther rode along without saying a word. For Slocum that was fine since he was lost in his own thoughts. The dustup between Wilson and Burning Tree had told Slocum it was time to ride on, but he was held back by wanting to see Mira. He doubted she would go with him since that meant leaving her family. Slocum doubted her attraction to him was that strong and he wasn't up to making any kind of a permanent arrangement with her.

"There's the wagon," Slocum said, spotting it where it had slid off the road ahead. The sun hammered the top of his head, forcing him to use some of his precious drinking water to douse himself for the moment of refreshing coolness it provided.

Luther slid from the back of the mule, went to the other one and began taking out his tools. He tossed them to the ground near the side of the wagon, took off his hat, scratched his head, then grunted like a pig.

"What is it?" Slocum took the sound to be some kind of communication from the man but he wasn't able to decipher it.

"Need rocks to hoist the wagon. What we gonna use to lift it?"

"Get the broken axle off," Slocum said. "We can use that for a lever."

"Oh, yeah," said Luther, setting to work. He might be good at fixing things but he lacked imagination.

Slocum climbed down from horseback and worked his way under the wagon to survey the damage. From his vantage he saw Luther's huge boots beside the wagon.

"You the new foreman, right?" asked the miner.

"Reckon so, since that's what Wilson said," Slocum replied, working at a dangling chain to free the broken axle.

"That means you get a share of the take, don't it?"

"No more 'n the rest of you." Slocum hadn't even heard what his new salary was supposed to be. Thirty dollars a month was hardly a wage to get rich on, but he couldn't complain that much. Wilson had given him the job when he had been flat broke and drifting down from the Truckee River, where he had made life miserable for a rancher over stray cattle. The rancher hadn't taken kindly to it and had sent his three sons to kill Slocum. Barely getting away, Slocum had decided the fight wasn't worth it. The rancher hadn't been right, but then Slocum hadn't been entirely in the right, either. Some fights aren't worth pursuing, and he had ridden south into Death Valley and had come on the Silver Emperor Mine.

"So you and me, we get the same cut?"

"Suppose so," Slocum said. "Wilson made me foreman, so might be I get more. Didn't ask."

He scooted out from under the wagon and brushed himself off.

"Grab the end of the axle and pull it out. There's the

rock that broke the axle. Use it to brace against, then we can lift the wagon up enough to get the wheel free."

Luther put his back to it while Slocum took off the locking nut on the wheel and rolled it away. They repeated the chore on the other side, giving Slocum the chance to see if the wheels were damaged. One rim was bent, making the wheel wobble when it spun. Otherwise, they were both usable.

It took the rest of the day to get rocks to prop up the wagon, run the new axle into place and reattach the wheels. The sun dipped low behind the Panamint Mountains when Slocum decided the wagon was fit enough to roll back to camp. They could work on it more there, to make certain the bent wheel rim didn't cause grief when the wagon carried a new load of silver.

"The new silver strike," Luther said. "We all get a share, right?"

"Hadn't heard," Slocum said. "I was in town getting supplies and wasn't long enough back in camp to hear."

"But we divvy it up equally? Maybe you get a bigger cut since you're foreman?"

Slocum looked at Luther in the gathering twilight and shook his head. This was the most the miner had said in a month. Maybe longer.

"You might be right," Slocum said, hoping this would stem the flow of words. He liked the hulking giant of a miner better when he kept his mouth shut.

"Whatya figure is in that mine?"

"The Silver Emperor? I can't say. I've been too busy breaking axles and going back and forth to Panamint City," Slocum said, his tone such that it ought to have stemmed any further discussion. To his surprise, it didn't. Luther pressed the matter.

"Each share might be a hundred dollars. Thass what ever' one's sayin'," the huge man said.

Slocum grunted noncommittally. He studied their handiwork and decided it was time to get back to camp.

"Hitch up the mules," Slocum said. "You know how to drive a wagon?"

"Course I do," Luther said. He opened his mouth to say something else, then clamped it shut. Slocum saw the mountain of a man working on what he had meant to say. "Been a while. Might be you should drive back."

"I'm not giving up my horse," Slocum said. "Besides, it's too tired to carry your weight."

"I kin ride in the wagon."

"Too much weight for a pair of mules," Slocum said, growing restive with this odd argument.

"Oh," Luther said, shrugging. He went to hitch up the mules and took his time. More than once he ran his hands over his jeans, as if getting rid of sweat. Slocum watched and wondered what was going on. He'd avoided Luther and most of the others, not so much because he didn't want their company but because he'd been busy with non-mining chores. From the day he had drifted into the mining camp, Wilson had set him to more important tasks. Like guarding the silver shipments. The last trip had been a disaster, losing both Benson and Zeb Matthews, but the silver bars had reached the bank to fund future expansion at the Silver Emperor.

"Get 'em moving," Slocum said, feeling edgy now. He had to tell Luther every move to make. "The mine's back that way, up the road going into Wildrose Canyon."

"Know that," Luther said sullenly. "Not stupid."

Slocum held his tongue. He was approaching the end of his rope with Luther but now that the wagon was repaired and on its way back to camp, he didn't have to spend any more time with him.

"I'll ride on ahead. You don't need me standing guard for you."

"What? You cain't!"

"Why not? Scared of the dark?"

"There, up ahead. See? Them's road agents, for sure. They're gonna kill me."

"What? Where?" Slocum rode forward and reined in next to the driver's box so he could get the same perspective on the road that Luther had. He saw nothing. He stood in the stirrups to get a better vantage. "Point them out. I don't see—"

Luther rose in the driver's box, stretched out and swung a wrench. Slocum was aware of the tool coming for him, tried to dodge and then felt the metal crunch hard into the side of his head. The world spun once, he was aware of falling and then darkness closed in on him.

5

Heat. Overwhelming heat hammered at John Slocum's back and legs. He stirred, moaned and tried to push to his hands and knees but he was too weak. He lay in the alkali dust, cheek enduring the grit until he summoned enough strength to try again. He succeeded this time, but a powerful lightning bolt of pain savaged his head and threatened to blast it apart. Dizzy, sick to his stomach, he stayed on his hands and knees for a minute or longer until he figured out what had happened.

"The son of a bitch," he grated out. "I'll kill you, Luther. Let me get my hands on you, and I swear I'll rip you apart with my bare hands!" He rocked back to sit on his heels, immediately noticing his silver spurs were missing. Slocum's hand patted himself down and found that he had been thoroughly robbed. His money was missing—and so was his brother Robert's watch.

The fury coursing through him now propelled him to his feet. His brother had been in Pickett's Charge, that ill-conceived, ultimately fatal attack that had left too many good Southern men dead and dying. Robert had been the cheerful brother, the one the girls flocked around because of his radiant good charm. John Slocum had been the expert hunter; Robert Slocum had been the farmer. And Robert had died, leaving behind as his legacy nothing

39

more than the watch Slocum jealously protected.

And it was gone.

His hand went to his left hip. Both his Colt Navy and gun belt were missing, too. The only bright spot in the robbery lay in the thief leaving him his life and a knife slid into the top of his boot.

"Luther, you're going to wish your mama had drowned you at birth." Slocum peered up at the intense sun beating down on Death Valley and estimated it was close to noon. It had been a little after sundown the night before when Luther had decoyed him and gotten him with the sucker blow. Call it fifteen hours.

He turned slowly, trying to figure out where he was. In all directions desert stretched to the horizons, now cloaked in shimmering silver heat haze. Slocum dropped to his knees and began crawling around, hunting for clues in the hard ground. He found the wagon tracks and the hoofprints beside it showing that Luther had brought him in the wagon and dumped him.

"He even stole my horse." Slocum shook his head, wondering how Luther would explain returning to camp with the repaired wagon and Slocum's horse. The man wasn't too swift and had to realize some story would be required if he showed up with Slocum's horse but not its rider.

"All for a few measly few dollars," Slocum said to himself, wiping the dust from his mouth. "A hell of an excuse to die for." He considered the direction Luther had driven and reckoned that way curled back toward the road to the Silver Emperor camp. On foot, it was too far. Exposed, in the middle of the dusty, sun-hardened flats, he would die before he reached the road.

Might be this is Mahogany Flat, he decided as he pulled up his bandanna to cover his nose and mouth. It did little to alleviate the growing thirst, but it kept some dust from getting in and turning his lips and tongue gummy. *Gotta find shelter. Gotta get out of the sun. Gotta.*

Slocum needed to head north to return to Wildrose Canyon, but that was too distant. Foothills to the east beckoned. He couldn't tell how far they were, but the promise of some shade drew him. In spite of Death Valley being so intensely hot, there were springs all over the terrain—for those who lived to find them. At Wildrose near the Modock kilns was a pool fed by a spring that pumped in better than two thousand gallons of sweet, cool water a day. Much of that was used by the hundred workers there, the kiln workers and the tree cutters who ventured as far as Telescope Peak for the wood. Slocum remembered Mira saying this wasn't even the largest of the springs, that many others popped up in odd places throughout the desert, mostly in the hillier sections.

This was an alkali flat and would never show a drop of water to a thirsty man. But the foothills to the east offered hope. There Slocum would find water. He had to or he would die.

Head down, eyes squinted against the intense sunlight, he put one foot in front of the other, plodding along, trying not to think of his misery. He was thirstier than he could remember ever being and his feet burned. Even through the thick leather soles of his boots, his feet sloshed through liquid fire with every step. Slocum knew he dared not stop, if he wanted to live. It soon became almost impossible to put even one foot in front of the other until he discovered that conjuring a mental image of Luther helped.

Fire from the sun and the desert coursed through his veins and gave him the determination required to keep moving.

More than a few times he had to lift his head and sight in on the distant hills. Men in a desert tended to circle slowly to the right. If he had maintained his head-down pace, this fate would have befallen him and he would have ended up heading back into the heart of the alkali flat. The hills were hazy. And he was never sure if it was a fading vision or the heat and dust. It didn't matter as long as he had the hills as a guidepost. The sun sank lower in the west, trying to hide behind the Panamint Mountains, but he was never quite released from the sun's fiery grip.

Slocum shuffled on, stumbling and falling to his knees more often now. The feel of Luther's neck under his fingers always got him back on his feet and lurching along until he caught a toe and fell facedown onto the ground. Stunned, he lay there for a moment trying to figure out what was different.

It was cooler now that the sun no longer spilled directly onto the crown of his hat, but there was something more.

"Rocks," he said in a barely audible voice. His tongue felt as if it had swelled to twice its usual size and his lips were caked and cracked in spite of the protective bandanna. But hope flared now. Rocks different from those in the flats rose in front of him. A slope. A steep slope.

He began crawling and found himself heading up a small hill. He had reached the foothills he had seen around midday. Scrabbling up, he reached the crest, then rolled over the top to find himself in glorious, cool darkness. Slocum lay on his back, staring at the darkening sky. It wasn't the black of night above him. It was some time until sunset, but he was out of the sun and the rocks under him had already given up their heat to provide revitalizing cool.

Trying to sit up too soon proved a failure, so he sank back and rested some more. He took off the bandanna and beat out a small dust cloud from it before tying it back around his gritty neck. Slocum noticed that he had stopped sweating. A bad sign. He needed water. Bad.

Rolling downhill rather than walking, he found that the far slope held heavier vegetation than the western slope. That made sense. The morning sun, as terrible as it was, lacked the knife-edged killing power of the afternoon. Patches of desert chicory and brittlebush told him there had to be water nearby. When a black-tailed jackrabbit hopped past, looking at him with the contempt of a desert dweller for the interloper, so he knew he was on the right track. A watering hole was nearby.

Thoughts jumbled and tumbled as he found a small game trail. From the droppings, larger animals frequented this trail, maybe as large as antelope. He also found scat from a fox. He was in no condition to trap or kill anything as cunning as a fox, and the jackrabbit had sized him up with easy contempt as not being a threat. Holding his hand out, Slocum saw how badly it shook.

He needed water. Now.

In the dusk he worried less about frightening off the animals he might need to live on than he did finding their watering hole. First things first. He could make a spear, tie his knife on the end of a short stick, use that to hunt.

So intent was he on finding water that he neglected to see the two Shoshones sitting on a rock overlooking the trail. Slocum had blundered past them. His first hint something was wrong was the soft movement of leather mocassin against rough rock. Then he was knocked forward and pinned to the ground.

The two hunters argued in their own language. Even as dazed as he was from his ordeal that day, Slocum knew the gist of the debate. He didn't try to get away; he was too weak for that. Instead, he bided his time, calculated how and when to move, did what he could to keep from having the air crushed from his lungs by the Indian kneeling in the middle of his back.

"Kill him!" shouted the one holding Slocum down.

When the other answered, possibly with a suggestion how best to accomplish this, Slocum shifted his weight to the right and waited for the Shoshone brave to respond. Then he heaved with all his strength to the left and gained a momentary advantage as the Indian lost his balance. Swarming up and back, Slocum got his knife out and shoved it at the brave's throat.

With contemptuous ease, the Shoshone grabbed Slocum's wrist and forced the hand back, then twisted and applied more pressure until the knife slipped from his numbed fingers. Then the Indian shoved him hard so he landed on the ground, out of breath.

The brave stood and peered down at his captive. The Indian's face was mostly hidden in shadow but Slocum read the triumph—and the contempt—in the way he stood. The

Shoshone detested weakness, and Slocum had failed to kill when he had tried.

"You gents know English?" Slocum tried to distract them to find another way of escaping death. He knew one spoke enough English to say "kill him" but Slocum wanted to divert him from that kind of thinking.

"You no belong here. Our land!"

"Right, your land," Slocum said, though his voice came out more as a croak than strong, confident words. He needed to show arrogance and disdain for them to reestablish his position. If he grovelled or they thought he remained weak, he was a goner. But his voice refused to cooperate.

"Kill him."

The brave standing over Slocum smiled, and it wasn't a pleasant expression. He drew a knife from his belt and, with a lightning-fast movement, threw the knife at Slocum. Slocum never flinched. The knife buried itself into the hard ground an inch away from his right ear. His green eyes bored into the Shoshone's dark eyes and showed not a hint of fear.

"Kill him!" cried the other. Since he spoke in English, Slocum knew both braves wanted him to know what they intended and to act scared. He might die, but he wasn't going to give them the satisfaction of seeing even a flicker of fear on his face.

Another voice rang down the narrow valley, sharp words in Shoshone Slocum did not understand. The man standing over him stepped back and looked toward the area where the watering hole had to be. Whatever had been said caused him to vent his ire. He rattled off a Gatling-gun–fast reply. Even angrier words replied. Slocum propped himself up on one elbow and saw a short man strutting up the trail, one he recognized immediately.

"I didn't think our paths would cross so soon, Burning Tree," Slocum said.

"Give Two-Toes back knife," Burning Tree said. "Now. No hurt you."

Slocum had plucked the brave's knife from the ground and had been ready to make another attack. Instead he tossed it clumsily in the direction of the one Burning Tree had called Two-Toes. The Indian caught the knife with disdainful ease and thrust it back into the sheath dangling at his belt, decorated with porcupine quills and several bird feathers.

It took almost all his strength, but Slocum got to his feet and held out his hand to Burning Tree. The Shoshone ignored it, choosing instead to stare defiantly at him. Slocum twigged to the situation right away. Burning Tree held some position of authority that would be ruined if he showed too much friendship with a white-eyes.

"Thanks," Slocum said simply. "Can I get my knife back?"

Burning Tree nodded once. Slocum bent, snatched up his knife and sheathed it in his boot before standing again. He was acutely aware of the two braves nearby, itching to kill him.

"Why you here?" demanded Burning Tree.

Slocum explained what had happened and what he hoped to get from the Shoshones. Burning Tree took it all in. Slocum wasn't sure how much the Indian understood, but it was enough.

Burning Tree reached out and gripped the back of Slocum's neck, pulling his head down to look at the spot where Luther had clubbed him. When the Indian touched the wound, Slocum flinched. It was a show of weakness, but he couldn't help it. The lance of pain that went through his head left him no choice.

Burning Tree yammered a few seconds to his two braves, who backed away, then they lightly ran toward the watering hole leaving Burning Tree and Slocum alone on the trail. Slocum stood silently, waiting for the Shoshone to give a hint what was expected.

"You have horse?"

"Stolen," Slocum said. "The miner who hit me took my horse, gun and watch." He hesitated, then added, "And my money."

Burning Tree nodded knowingly. The horse, gun and money meant more to the Indian than the watch. To Slocum, he would trade them all to get his brother's timepiece back. He stood and waited some more. It was always like this dealing with Indians. They had their own sense of time and when decisions had to be made.

After what seemed an eternity, Burning Tree said, "You eat. You drink. Leave then."

"That suits me," Slocum said. "Are you the big chief?" He made a sweeping motion to encompass the entire land, then pointed in the direction of the watering hole. All he got from Burning Tree was a sharp snort that might have been derisive or even agreement to the idea he was a chief. Slocum couldn't tell which it was.

"Come," Burning Tree said after a spell. He walked silently down the path to the pool of water, sheltered by low-growing sage and taller creosote bushes. Across the pond sat a dozen Shoshone hunters, all with silent eyes turned to Slocum. He did not acknowledge their presence. To have done so would complicate his position—whatever that might be. He trailed Burning Tree to a spot where a small fire pit had been dug into the muddy shore. A rabbit had been roasted some time back. If Slocum had caught the scent on the wind, he would have come straight here, but from the look of the cold, greasy carcass, Burning Tree had fixed the meal some hours earlier.

Burning Tree pointed. Slocum hunkered down, grabbed the rabbit and ate until he choked. He went to the pond and cupped water, brining it to his lips. Between the two, food or water, he needed the liquid more. He drank his fill, then returned to the rabbit until he had picked the bones clean. He dropped the gnawed skeleton into the shallow pit, then kicked dirt over it to erase all trace of the fire or the meal.

The Indian fiddled with something. Only when a glint of moonlight from the sliver in the sky caught the edge of the coin did Slocum figure out what Burning Tree had in his hand. It was one of the three cartwheels he had given the Indian in payment for his help getting the supplies back to the Silver Emperor Mine.

"Go now," Burning Tree said suddenly. "Take this. Go." He picked up a jar and thrust it into Slocum's hands.

Slocum quickly filled the jar with water, drank a bit more, washed out his bandanna and hung it soaking around his neck, then set out silently. The water wouldn't last him long but if he walked fast during the night, he wouldn't freeze and he could get close to the Silver Emperor camp. Come sunrise, he'd cut Luther from the herd and give him what for.

That thought kept him moving all night long.

6

An hour before dawn Slocum dropped wearily onto a rock and surveyed the Silver Emperor mining camp. Somewhere in there, probably sound asleep in one of the bunkhouses, lay Luther. The thought of the bushwhacking son of a bitch sent Slocum's heart pumping faster. Blood raced through his veins and burned away the exhaustion from walking all night to get here. If it hadn't been for Burning Tree, he might have ended up dead. Slocum wasn't sure if they were even, but if the Shoshone ever asked a favor of him again, Slocum was mighty sure he would oblige.

But he had a chore to tend to right now. An unpleasant one.

He got to his feet and walked down the road into the camp. Two sentries spotted him and waved.

"Hey, Slocum, where you been? Luther said you'd gone off with a bunch of sodbusters wantin' a scout."

"Life with sodbusters is too dull," Slocum said, keeping his anger in check. "Where's Luther? I need to have a word with him."

The two guards came over and looked closer at him, then exchanged looks. Both turned a mite frightened. Slocum had not said anything, but his demeanor was enough to put the fear of God into the best of them.

"You got a bone to pick with 'im?" asked one.

48

"He . . . borrowed something of mine. I want it back."

"H-he's likely still sleepin'," said the second guard. "You want us to go fetch him?"

"This is personal."

"We can't have no trouble. Look, Slocum, Mr. Wilson he tole us to keep things nice and quiet, 'specially after last night."

Slocum stared at the man, not knowing what he meant.

"The champagne. We drunk it all up. Most of the fellas, they got mighty soused, you know what I mean? Rowdy? They busted up some of the equipment and each other and Mr. Wilson don't want that happenin' no more."

"I won't bust up any equipment," Slocum said. "And I'm stone-cold sober."

"Uh, why don't you go report to Mr. Wilson?"

"Where's Luther?" He spoke so softly the two men took a step back and looked around as if fearing for their lives. "You boys have nothing to worry about. It's Luther I want. Just him. Nobody else, unless they stand in my way."

"Whatever you say, Slocum. You want us to tell him you're here?"

"I'll do it myself. Which bunkhouse?" Slocum saw both men point to the same one. He reckoned that meant they told the truth and were too frightened to lie. His long stride took him to the bunkhouse in jig time and he went inside, his sharp gaze hunting for Luther. He didn't see him but came upon an empty bunk.

"This one Luther's?" he asked no one in particular. Two men in nearby bunks stirred. One grunted assent. Slocum began pawing through Luther's gear and found his six-shooter right away. He strapped on the cross-draw holster and settled it, then rammed the ebony-handled Colt Navy in. It felt good weighing him down again, but he was happy that he hadn't had to lug it across Death Valley to get here.

He separated his gear from Luther's and stood back. His watch wasn't in the saddlebags or hidden under the pillow or thin pallet where Luther slept.

"Where'd he get off to?"

The two guards stood in the doorway. One cleared his throat and pointed toward the rear of the bunkhouse, silently showing where Luther had gone.

"To the outhouse?" Slocum saw both guards nodding as if their necks had been replaced with springs. He made sure his six-shooter was loaded, then slid it back into the holster before going to the rear door and kicking it open. The sound brought even the deepest sleeper among the miners fully awake and complaining. Slocum ignored them and stalked out.

Ahead of him a ways downhill stood the solitary outhouse. The door was partially ajar and he saw movement inside. Slocum tapped his fingers on the handle of his six-gun but did not draw. Aware of the two guards and several of the miners slipping out of the bunkhouse behind him, he doubted he could get by with shooting a man while he attended a call to Nature, as much as that man deserved it.

Besides, Slocum wanted his watch back. If he shot Luther while he was tending to his business, he might put a slug right through it by accident.

Slocum walked forward. A gasp rose among the onlookers. But Slocum didn't draw. He kicked out powerfully and sent the rickety outhouse rocking. A second kick knocked it over. Looking up from his seat, eyes wide in surprise, was Luther.

"Slocum!"

"Didn't figure on seeing me again, did you?" Slocum took another step forward and smashed the clay pot Burning Tree had given him for water against Luther's forehead. The man rocked to one side and then went rolling downhill, his pants still around his ankles. Slocum followed him down the slope and found him wrapped around a chamisa bush, struggling to get up. Slocum measured his distance and kicked as hard as he could. The toe of his boot connected with Luther's midriff. The shock went all the way up Slocum's leg to his hips. It was like kicking a rock.

"Whadya doin' this fer?" Luther struggled to get his pants up but sitting on the ground made it difficult.

"Where's my watch? The one you stole off me?"

"I ain't got no watch."

"Then you're a dead man," Slocum said. Luther looked up and saw the tombstone mirrored in Slocum's eyes—his own tombstone.

"This ain't right. You cain't go—"

Slocum kicked him again, this time in the chest. Again he felt the impact with the starkly muscled body, but his anger knew no bounds.

"My watch. It belonged to my brother. Give me my watch back. I already took my gun and gear. What about the money you took, too? And my spurs."

"You got this all wrong, Slocum," said Luther, finally pulling up his pants and sliding his arms through the suspenders to hold them up.

"You're the one who got it wrong," Slocum said, "thinking you could dry-gulch me, steal my belongings and leave me to die in the middle of the desert."

A gasp went up behind Slocum. He was speaking to the crowd, letting them know it would be a damn fool thing on their part to meddle.

"Hell, Slocum, it was like I said. Luther there tole us you'd gone off with sodbusters."

"They got that wrong. Never said any sich thing," Luther muttered, looking like a child with his hand caught in the cookie jar.

"Give me the watch."

"Or what?" Luther showed a flare of anger, figuring Slocum wasn't going to shoot him out of hand with so many witnesses. Luther went pale when Slocum drew his pistol in a quick, smooth movement, then swung the barrel and clipped him on the side of the head. The loud *thunk!* echoed across the camp, and Luther fell back to the ground, stunned.

"My watch."

Luther made a small gesture toward a watch pocket in his jeans. Slocum dropped down, his knee going into Luther's belly as he gripped the edge of the pocket and then ripped as hard as he could. The cloth came off and the watch popped out like a mesquite bean from its pod. Slocum held up the watch and looked at it in the faint light of dawn. Satisfied that his brother's watch still worked, he tucked it into his vest pocket where it had ridden since the war.

Slocum rocked back and stood, pointed his six-shooter directly at Luther's head. The hammer came back with a metallic click, but Slocum hesitated.

"Shooting you's too good," he said, lowering the hammer and then cramming his six-shooter back into its holster. He stripped off his gun belt and held it out. One of the miners behind him hastily took it.

"This, too," Slocum said, passing over the watch.

"I'll look after it real good, Slocum," the miner said in a voice more like a croaking bullfrog.

"Get to your feet." Slocum's anger did not die down. It grew like some festering wound that spread throughout his body, but Luther misinterpreted the extent of Slocum's rage. He got to his feet, a crooked grin on his ugly face.

"You want a piece of me, Slocum? Come on. Come and git it!"

Slocum wasn't suckered into getting close enough for Luther to grab him in a deadly bear hug that would snap his back like a twig. He had kicked the man and felt the slabs of muscle. Slocum knew he was up against a strong opponent, but he also knew Luther didn't have two brain cells to rub together.

Slocum's fist shot out like a striking snake and lightly brushed across Luther's cheek. The giant of a man recoiled more from surprise than from injury. With a mighty roar, he launched himself at Slocum, intending to wrestle. Slocum got in three hard blows to the belly, swung to the side and kicked out, tripping Luther. The giant fell face-down in the dust, shoved himself to his hands and knees and let Slocum plant another kick to his exposed belly.

Luther grunted and shrugged off the blow, but Slocum circled. He knew another chance would come. And it did. Luther rushed him again. Slocum shot out a pair of hard punches to the area around Luther's heart, staggering him. But this time he was too slow getting out of the huge man's way. Powerful hands clamped on Slocum's shoulder and spun him around.

Then he was lifted off the ground in the embrace he feared most. Slocum's only saving grace was that Luther had his clenched fists in the pit of his stomach, not the small of his back. Luther applied immense pressure in his attempt to break Slocum in two, but he hadn't counted on Slocum's determination for revenge.

With a powerful kick, Slocum unbalanced Luther. Then he bent forward, reached behind him and grabbed a double handful of long, stringy hair. Using every ounce of energy in his body, Slocum heaved and Luther went flying over his shoulder to land on the ground. Slocum kept his grip on the man's hair with one hand and pummeled him with the other. Only when one of Luther's eyes began to swell did Slocum back off to regain his breath.

The fight was harder than he thought it would be. His ribs had been bruised, but the knot in the pit of his stomach where Luther had clutched him hurt like hell.

"I'll kill you, Slocum. I oughta kilt you before, but I went soft."

"You're so stupid you couldn't kill me even when I was knocked out," Slocum said. "What makes you think you'll be able to do it now?"

Luther let out a bull roar as he charged. Slocum feinted to the left, went right and tripped him. Luther crashed to the ground like a felled tree, but this time he didn't let Slocum get close enough to kick him again.

"You're a dead man, Slocum."

"You've already had your chance and you blew it," Slocum said, calculating what it would take to end Luther's miserable life. He stepped up, fists cocked back as he waited for an opening. Luther gave it to him right away. Slocum unleashed a furious barrage of punches, all aimed at Luther's heart. When the man finally reacted—it took a long time for the messages of pain to reach his pea-sized brain—Luther swung a haymaker that landed on Slocum's shoulder.

Staggering away, his arm momentarily numb from the Herculean blow, Slocum felt his guard drop slightly as his left arm throbbed from the battering ram punch he had taken. Luther took this as a chance to attack. Slocum couldn't respond with his fists so he kicked out again, this time connecting with Luther's kneecap.

The dull *snap!* told of important bones breaking. Luther cried in pain and staggered past Slocum. With his good hand Slocum punched several more times, trying to land them all around Luther's heart.

"You hurt me," Luther cried. The fury on the man's face told the story. Slocum had to do something fast or the fight would be over—and he would be dead.

Rubbing his arm until the circulation returned, Slocum measured his opponent and saw the way he moved, how he favored his left side where most of the strongest punches had come from. When Luther lumbered forward in attack again, Slocum put his head down and went in swinging. His fists pounded furiously, getting past Luther's feeble guard. When Slocum thought the bones in his hands would break from hammering so hard against Luther's chest, he redoubled his efforts. Then he drew back and uncorked a blow that came from a mile off. His right fist crushed into Luther's chest directly over the heart.

Luther let out a tiny gasp, his knees buckled and he crashed to the ground without another sound.

"Glory be, Slocum, you knocked him out," marvelled a miner.

Doc Lonigan pushed through the crowd and rolled Luther over onto his back. He put his finger under the fallen man's nose, then ripped open the filthy union suit covering Luther's chest. The flesh over Luther's heart had turned to a black and purple swamp. Lonigan looked up and said, almost in awe, "He's dead. You hit him so hard, you burst his heart!"

Slocum stood and stared at Luther's corpse. He felt no triumph.

"He got what he deserved for dry-gulching me the way he did."

"He slugged Slocum and then upped and left him out in the desert," piped up a miner. "Slocum here came after him 'cuz he stole his watch."

"And ever'thin' else," supplied another miner.

"Never seen a man beat to death like that, especially one Luther's size," opined another.

The miners came by and slapped Slocum on the back. He stood and stared down at the body, wishing there had been more. He unclenched his fists and felt pain jet up into his forearms.

"Here, Slocum, take 'em," said a miner who thrust out Slocum's watch and six-shooter.

"Thanks. Reckon I ought to tell Wilson what happened," Slocum said.

"You might want to soak them hands in ice water to keep 'em from swelling up too much," Doc Lonigan said. "I can tell him all he needs to know."

"Thanks, Doc, but this is still my concern." He started toward the small shack some distance from camp where Big Pete Wilson slept.

"Slocum!" called Lonigan. "If you get fired, it's been good knowin' you."

Slocum laughed without humor and plodded toward Wilson's shack, suddenly finding it almost impossible to stay on his feet. He planted himself squarely in front of the door and knocked until Wilson came to the door. When it opened Wilson stared at him without really seeing him, then blinked.

"You back?"

"I had business to tend to," Slocum said, holding up his skinned knuckles.

"What are you talkin' about? Luther said you—"

"Luther's dead," Slocum said. There wasn't any cause to pour syrup on it. "I whupped him in a fair fight."

"You beat him to death? Luther Wykowsky? He was built like a damned bull!"

"All that means is it'll be harder to dig a grave because it has to be bigger."

"You killed him?"

Slocum explained why. Wilson's eyes slowly got wider and his mouth flopped open a couple times, only to snap shut.

"So if you want to fire me, go on."

"Fire you!" cried Wilson. "I ought to have you arrested." Wilson settled down and asked, "Why'd Luther do that to you? You said you didn't have that much money."

"He figured you were going to give equal shares to all the men from the new silver strike. If I'm dead, his cut would be bigger."

Wilson shook his head. "Luther never was much of a thinker. You reckon he really thought he'd make that much more? Why not kill everyone else?"

"You have any other men go missing recently?"

From the shocked expression on Wilson's face, Slocum knew the answer.

When Wilson found his voice, he said, "I ought to give you a raise. You might have saved me the loss of other good men."

"So I'm still on the payroll?"

"As my foreman," Wilson declared. "And you take the day off. You deserve it."

Slocum was past thanking his boss. He could hardly raise his arms and his step was leaden, but he knew how he'd spend his day off and where he'd get the medicine he needed to feel better.

7

"You ever want to go into bare-knuckle fighting, Slocum," said Doc Lonigan, "I'll consider it an honor to be in your corner. But you got to soak them hands in saltwater before the fight. Makes the skin tougher and deadens the pain." Lonigan held up Slocum's hand and examined it in the morning sun. The miners had been at their work underground for more than an hour, and Slocum had slept late, until well after dawn. The gathering heat had forced him from the bunkhouse, and the pain in his hands had made him seek out Lonigan.

"Anything more you can do for them now?"

Lonigan shook his head, then chuckled. "Wait a second. I got just the thing." He rummaged in his supplies and produced a champagne bottle. "Take a long draw on that. It's not bad, but it's not champagne, either."

Slocum almost choked when he took a pull.

"Strong, ain't it?" Lonigan laughed. "The swill you brought back was nothing compared to some hooch an old gent up in the hills makes. I bought his entire production, what he didn't drink himself."

"That's powerful stuff," Slocum said, putting down the bottle.

"Have another drink. You won't feel a thing."

"That's because I'll be on the ground, just like I got kicked in the head by a mule."

Lonigan laughed again, took the bottle and availed himself of a long drink. He gulped, then wiped his lips with his sleeve.

"Yes, sir, this is the real stuff. Not the dog piss you brought back."

Slocum flexed his hands and winced at the pain, but he felt the warmth in his belly spreading throughout his body. The moonshine whiskey was having its effect.

"Don't go gettin' into any more fights, and be real careful if you have to go for that hogleg of yours. Your fingers might not curl just right, not for a day or two."

Slocum practiced a draw and saw what Lonigan meant. He was just a tad clumsy because of the beating his hands had taken.

"See you this evening, or maybe tomorrow morning," Slocum said, putting his hat on to protect his head from the sun.

"Going out to scout the territory?" asked Lonigan, lounging back and taking another sip of his bootleg whiskey. "Or should I say *her* territory?"

"Don't make me find out how much more it'd hurt if I had to whup up on you, Doc." Slocum flexed his hand.

"Go on, get out of here. I envy you, Slocum. You not only got the only woman for miles around, you got the purtiest one in all of California. Me, I have to console my lonely old bones with a smooth, green-skinned young lady called tarantula juice." He stroked up and down the neck of the champagne bottle, then raised it in mock salute.

Slocum went to the corral and cut out his horse. He wondered what story Luther had told about returning with the horse, then shrugged it off. Nobody had much cared or even noticed the discrepancy of a man supposedly going to scout for a party of sodbusters and Luther returning with his horse. Life was hard in Death Valley and even harder in the silver mine. Nobody questioned anything too much.

Slocum rode slowly from the Silver Emperor camp

down the road cut through the middle of Wildrose Canyon.
The charcoal kilns were at the far end, close to where trees
had grown at one time. Now the woodcutters had to fan out
and find their trees at ever higher altitudes in even more re-
mote locations.

The kilns were distinctive even at a distance, standing
more than twenty-five feet tall. Mira had told him each of
the monster furnaces could burn more than forty cords of
piñon and, after a week of cooking, produce more than two
thousand bushels of charcoal. Left to his own devices and
avarice, Big Pete Wilson would have bought the whole lot,
but the kilns supplied more than a half dozen other mines,
including those owned by George Hearst.

The heavy burning odor drifted downwind to Slocum
and made his nose wrinkle. The kilns were stoked and
making a new batch of the material needed most to separate silver from its ore. Slocum's attention was fixed on the
row of ten kilns ahead but movement at the edge of his vision caused him to draw rein and look around.

Two men rode along the canyon rim. This wasn't un-
usual so near the kilns, but the way they rode put Slocum
on guard. Honest men had no need to act as furtively as
these two did. One caught sight of him down on the canyon
floor, called to his partner and they both vanished. Slocum
fished out a pair of binoculars from his saddlebags, wiped
off the lenses, then lifted them to his eyes and waited.

Less than five minutes later, the pair reappeared, thinking he had ridden on. Slocum tried to get a better look at
their faces, but the distance was still too great. When they
spotted him watching them, they applied their spurs to
their horses and raced off. He put the binoculars away and
wondered what mischief these two were up to. As he rode,
a thought came to him.

There might be a great wealth of silver shipped from
Death Valley into Panamint City and beyond, but there was
another "gold" mine and it lay ahead. The difference was
that this mine didn't produce precious metal but crumbly
black charcoal. Nobody would steal a wagonload of char-

coal just for the charcoal; but charcoal fetched good prices, paid in silver. There might be a considerable hoard of payment for the product hidden away in the kilns.

"Hey, Slocum, good to see you," called a stoker on the kilns. He wiped away sweat and left a black streak on his forehead. "She's not in camp right now."

"Damn," Slocum said. "Does everybody know my business?"

"And Miss Mira's," said the workman, laughing. "What else we got to gossip about out here in the middle of nowhere?"

"Where is she?" Slocum hoped she hadn't gone into Panamint City. There wasn't any good way of chasing after her and spending any time with her if she was out of camp.

"Down by the pond. She's got some ridiculous idea she can use charcoal to get the shit outta water. Hell, if it don't choke ya when you drink it, how can it hurt you?"

"By the pond, you say?" Slocum was already riding down the winding path leading to the large pond supplying the water for the entire camp of a hundred workers as the words slipped from his mouth. He didn't want to seem too eager, but he was. He had been through hell during the past couple days and was ready for a little piece of heaven.

He stopped and looked around when he came to the large pond. For Death Valley it might count as a lake, but the size was nothing compared to lakes he knew in the Rockies or even the nearby Sierra Nevadas. Still, it was a powerful lot more water than anywhere else he knew, fed by springs and crystal clear. Slocum started to call out for Mira but held back when he saw her about a quarter of the way around the lake, kneeling at the shore and dipping water out to pour into a bucket. He dismounted and led his horse away from the water, a difficult thing to do because the horse's nostrils had flared once it realized it was near so much water.

"Soon, soon," he soothed the horse as he led it into the thin wooded area behind where Mira worked. The trees weren't fit for use as charcoal, mostly being soft wood pines. He came up behind the crouching woman and stopped a few yards away, appreciating the view from this angle. Then his horse tossed its head and jerked the reins out of his still sore hands and trotted to the pond.

Mira jumped as if someone had stuck her with a pin. She dropped the bucket, half stood, lost her balance and fell into the water, sitting ungracefully.

"Don't you usually take off your clothes when you take a bath?" asked Slocum, grinning broadly at the sight. The water had plastered Mira's clothing to her, causing her ample breasts to look as if they were bare. Her legs were drawn up, and her skirt had fallen back around her waist, giving a delicious view of the waves licking against her most intimate regions. She saw how he took note and widened her legs a little more and rocked back, supporting herself on her elbows.

"So?"

"You're about the prettiest sight I've seen," Slocum said, not moving.

"About? I'm *about* the prettiest thing? You'd better change your tune fast, mister."

"You *are* the prettiest woman I've ever seen," Slocum said, "and I've never seen another woman fish for compliments like you."

"Must be because I'm flopping around in the water like a fish," Mira said. She dropped flat onto her back and splashed furiously, startling Slocum's horse. He grabbed the reins and led the horse back to a shady spot where it could find some thin grass to nibble while he was otherwise occupied.

"Well? Are you going to rescue me?"

"I'll throw you a line," Slocum said, returning to the bank and removing his gun belt.

"A line? I don't want a line. I want your pole!" Mira Van Winkle kicked her legs up high into the air so her skirt bunched around her waist, giving Slocum an arousing view.

"You're not wearing any undies," he said, tossing his shirt to the ground and kicking out of his boots.

"And I'm not wearing a skirt now, either," she said,

wiggling about as she pulled the skirt down in a wet lump. Naked from the waist down, she gleamed in the hot desert sun but she wasn't content with this and kept going, discarding her blouse, too. Then Mira kicked about, got to her knees and made a clean dive into deeper water. Slocum felt himself responding powerfully to the sight of her bare white rump appearing above the water and then disappearing.

Mira surfaced and shook her long, dark hair from her face. Her bright blue eyes rivaled the Death Valley sky, but there he found only life and merriment. No clouds, nothing but a lust that matched his own.

He got out of his jeans, took a few steps, then dived into the pond. The cold water took his breath away—and more.

"Oh, you lost it," Mira said, paddling over to him in deeper water and reaching down between his legs. "Is the nasty ole cold water doing that to you? Or did you decide you didn't like me any more?"

Her rhythmic squeezing and the sight of her breasts bobbing inches away, pink nipples just under the water and magnified to twice their real size sent a jolt of pure desire through Slocum's body and into his manhood. He stiffened again, in spite of the cold water.

"That's more like it," Mira said, using her grip on him to pull them closer. Slocum grunted but did not protest because Mira closed her blue eyes and parted her ruby lips just a little.

He kissed her. She released her warm hold on his member and threw her arms about his neck. At the same time she opened her legs and got them wrapped around his waist so they were pressed tightly together, at breast and groin and lips. Their kiss deepened as they spun around and around in the water. Slocum felt as if he had taken another swig of Doc Lonigan's potent firewater. Every nerve in his body exploded with heat but this didn't rely on alcohol. It was making him drunk with desire.

"You surely do know how to kiss, Mr. Slocum. That's one thing I like about you."

"What's another?"

"Oh? And who's fishing for compliments now? Let me tell you, that pole of yours isn't long enough to catch many fish." She dived beneath the surface and he felt her lips brush the tip of his rigid length. Then she enmouthed him and licked and stroked with her eager, active tongue until he wanted to explode. When he was sure he couldn't contain himself another instant, she surfaced and paddled away a few feet.

"Where you going?"

"I said that pole wasn't long enough to catch a real fish. If you don't agree, prove it!" Laughing, Mira rolled onto her belly and began swimming away fast, heading for the middle of the pond. It took Slocum a few seconds to realize she wanted him to chase her. He sucked in a deep breath, kicked powerfully and began swimming. He found that in his aroused condition this was harder than it ought to be.

"You've got an advantage on me," he called. "It feels like I've got something holding me back."

"Oh, do you now? It's *that* big and holding you back? Why not use it as a rudder?" she taunted. Mira came up out of the water so far he saw her from the waist up. And just below the waterline he caught sight of a fleecy black triangle of matted fur that made him even harder.

She splashed back and vanished. The next thing he knew he felt her lips on him again, this time working all around his iron-hard shaft. She sucked the hairy bag underneath into her mouth and tongued it for a second, then simply . . . vanished.

Slocum floated on his back, then turned over agilely in the water and dived, hunting for her. Mira proved more elusive than he expected. Deeper and deeper he went in the pond until he came to the bottom, but nowhere in the clear water did he see the sleek young woman. Then he looked up at the surface and saw her long legs slowly scissoring back and forth invitingly. Lungs almost bursting, Slocum shot straight up, aiming for the vertex of those lovely legs.

He heard Mira let out a squeal of joy when he rose and

pressed his mouth into the furry tangle. His tongue lashed out and gave her as much pleasure as she had already given him, then he twisted about and came to the surface, gasping for air.

"You're making me breathless," he said, sputtering and sending a spray of water into the air.

"Good," she said, lurching partially up out of the water and crashing down on him. For a moment they both went underwater in a froth of movement. When they surfaced, Slocum definitely liked the way they were docked. He was firmly inserted into her moist, hot core and her legs once more wrapped around him to hold them both in place.

"Oh, John," she sighed. "That feels so heavenly."

He bucked, arching his back and then pushing his butt back down into the water. This moved him within her tightness just a little. The expression on Mira's face turned to one of stark passion. She reached out and clung tenaciously to him as they rolled and bucked and frolicked in the water, all the time locked together at the groin.

As thrilling as it was, Slocum felt the pressures mounting within for more. In the water, he couldn't get the proper leverage or power for what he wanted to do. What he had to do.

By mutual silent agreement they drifted toward the shore, stroking over each other's body, teasing and kissing and stimulating all the little places while remaining joined. Both were panting with excitement by the time they reached the sandy shoreline. Mira ended up beneath him, her legs parting wantonly in invitation. Slocum scooted up out of the water until it lapped at his upper thighs. He felt the wetness surging back and forth around their crotches, stimulating them with wet fingers.

But when Mira's knees lifted on either side of his body, he moved forward forcefully. He sank far into her clinging, soft wetness, paused a moment to take in the full sensation, then pulled back slowly. Every inch pushed their desires higher.

"You're so . . . big," she gasped out. "You fill me up so, John. More, give me more. More!"

She let out a shriek that must have been heard throughout Death Valley. Slocum never slowed when he thrust forward, then pulled back and repeated the powerful movement. He turned into a human piston, moving slickly, easily, with increasing need and desire. Mira quivered under him, causing her breasts to jiggle about. He bent low and lightly kissed them, then bit and licked and did what he could. But the real action burned at his waist, in his loins, deep within.

The pressures mounted, and Slocum only vaguely was aware of how Mira continued to shake and moan and then arch her back as she tried to get him even deeper within. He maintained the steady movement until he reached the point of no return. He was aware of how she cried out again and clung to him, her fingers raking his back. Heat from the sun, blood from her clawing, the wind blowing hotly across the pond, the water, the warmth surrounding his manhood, it all pushed him over the edge. He erupted. His hips swung forward as he tried to bury himself entirely within Mira.

The white-hot syrupy mixture hidden inside him blasted outward, and then the moment of joy passed and he sank down on Mira.

"You're sweating," she said in a low voice. Mira craned her neck and kissed his cheeks, licked his forehead and down the side, toyed with his ear and finally ended with a deep, passionate kiss on the lips. "And you taste good, too."

Slocum worked his hands underneath Mira's pert, round rump and heaved, rolling her over and over until they were splashing about in the water again.

They romped like kids for a while and then floated about in the pond until Mira said, "We'd better get out. The sun's going to fry us."

"We wouldn't want certain parts getting sunburned, would we?" Slocum said. He laughed when she reached over and grabbed him between the legs again.

"I can keep this from getting burned. All you need to do is find a place to hide it from the sun."

"Where's that?"

"Well," Mira said, grinning wickedly, "if you have to ask . . ."

Slocum wrapped his arms around her and swung her about in the water to get a better look at the trees where he had tethered his horse. Movement. A man. Men!

"Somebody's watching us," he said.

"Oh, it's probably Ollie. I've caught him spying on me when I was undressing a couple times. I'd tell my pa, but Ollie's a good worker."

"There're a couple of them. Unless Ollie's got a friend—" Slocum cut off his words when he felt his feet on the slick bottom of the pond. He dug in his toes and launched himself, half falling as he rocketed from the water. He rolled to the side, grabbed his six-shooter and came to his feet. He was aware he was stark naked, but the Colt Navy in his grip made up for the lack of clothing. With long strides, he went to where his horse uneasily jerked on the reins. Something had spooked the animal, and Slocum saw instantly that he hadn't been wrong. Bootprints in the grass showed where the men had come up, stood for a few minutes, then retreated.

He started after them when Mira called from the pond.

"John, please, come back. Don't!"

Being naked was a drawback, but he had six bullets to cover his indecent appearance. But Mira sounded so forlorn that he hesitated.

"John! Don't. *Please*!"

He looked through the sparse stand of trees and didn't see the men. They couldn't be more than a few minutes ahead of him, but his nakedness began to worry him more and more.

"John!"

"I'm coming," he said, retracing his footsteps and dropping to the sandy shore. He pulled on his jeans, then his boots, although he doubted he could follow the men over the hard baked desert beyond the trees, beyond the kilns. By now they could be a mile off.

"You don't have to go after them," Mira said, rising out of the water like some Greek goddess. Water droplets sparkled like diamonds on her white skin and gave him pause. Then he grabbed his shirt and began pulling it on, difficult as that was because of his wet arms and chest.

"I saw them before, when I was riding down the canyon to the kilns. I watched them with my field glasses for a spell, and they were mighty furtive. I think they might be outlaws."

"Members of the Mojave Guns," she said.

"Could be." Then he stared at her. Mira hadn't suggested they might be. She had flat-out said they were.

"You know them," Slocum said. She nodded. She began wringing out her clothing and getting dressed. "Who are they?"

"Like I said. They ride with the Mojave Guns." She turned her blue eyes to him. He saw tears welling in the corners of those bright eyes when she said, "One's named Avery Caudell. The other . . . the other's my brother, Rafe."

8

Slocum looked at Mira Van Winkle and wondered why she had so readily admitted her brother was an outlaw. For most families, having a black sheep meant hiding the fact, talking about anything else, even disowning the miscreant loudly and often. That might be where she was headed with her bold statement.

"Rafe is a good man, but he fell in with a bad crowd."

"I've heard that song before," Slocum said in disgust. He had never ridden with a gang of road agents that didn't have at least one member whose only conversation was how he had been forced into robbing by chance. Slocum had always been honest about his thievery. If he rode with outlaws, he did it for a reason: money. Sometimes there was nothing to be proud of when he did it, but he had never lied or tried to convince himself that he stole because of others forcing him into it.

"You don't know how it is."

"You'd be surprised," he said, looking around. "Is there a reward on his head?"

"I reckon there might be. You intend to be the bounty hunter bringing him in?" She sat in the blazing sun, letting the heat dry her clothing to her body. Slocum heaved a deep sigh. She was mighty pretty, and maybe the finest woman he had come across in a month of Sundays.

"I'm not going after him, but he's likely to end up with one of my bullets in him if he tries to rob any of the Silver Emperor shipments. Wilson hired me to guard them and get them through to Panamint City. If Rafe tries to rob me, I won't have any choice." Slocum hesitated, then laid his cards on the table. "In a shoot-out, who do you think is more likely to walk away?"

"You," Mira said in a small voice. "Rafe's not all that good with a gun. Why, he hardly can stay on his horse. He's a real greenhorn."

"Then it's time he took a job working for your pa at the kilns 'fore he ends up in an unmarked grave in some potter's field." Slocum closed his eyes for a moment, thinking of Zeb Matthews's grave. And Bennie Benson's, too. They had died for nothing—at the hands of the Mojave Guns. Might be Rafe Van Winkle had been responsible, at least partly, since neither man would have died if the outlaws hadn't attacked the silver wagon.

"He won't do that. He and Pa had a big falling out. Besides, Rafe'd see working here as being *my* employee. He'd never take to working for a woman."

"He's not got his head screwed on straight, then," Slocum said. "You tell him what he's up against." With a slight shrug of his shoulders, Slocum had his Colt Navy out, cocked and aimed at Mira. Her eyes widened in surprise.

"You're fast," she said in her choked voice. "I didn't even see a blur when you dragged that gun out of the holster."

"I'm usually faster. Right now I got me some bruised knuckles that slow me down," Slocum said, not bragging too much. The bruises on his hands were a nuisance, but he had worked out the stiffness now. The lovemaking with Mira had been a big incentive to get his hands moving so he could fondle and feel, probe and stoke all over her fine body.

"I don't know if I'll see Rafe," Mira said.

"Tell him what I said. If he wants to be a road agent, let him move on. There are plenty of other places with rich mines."

"But none where Big Pete Wilson is owner!" she blurted.

"What's that got to do with it?"

"I . . . I said too much. Forget it, John." Mira turned away, tears running down her cheeks. She covered quickly by scooping up a handful of water and splashing it on her face. "You'd better go. I have to get back to work, and I suspect you do, too."

"They said you were trying to clean up water by using charcoal. What's that got to do with work?"

"That? Oh, just an idea I had. I noticed how running water through charcoal cleans it of all kinds of things. Crushed up charcoal, that is. I reckoned we might get better-tasting water if we tried filtering it."

"Never heard of such a thing. My idea of filtering water's to run it through my handkerchief to get out the big lumps."

Mira laughed but it wasn't heartfelt. "I can get out tiny things, too, too small to see. I even have a microscope back at my bunk. There're all kinds of wiggly little things in water. I can get rid of some of them using crushed charcoal but I—" Mira cut off her lecture when she saw Slocum looking around, into the woods, along the trail taken by her brother and Avery Caudell.

"Get on with it," Slocum said. "If the water gets too bad, I can always boil it."

"But with this filter, if it works the way I think it will, you won't have to—" Mira heaved a sigh. Slocum appreciated the way her breasts rose, fell and jiggled just a little, but his mind had moved on to other things. Like her outlaw brother and the gang he rode with.

He gave Mira a quick kiss good-bye, got his horse and walked it around to the road leading to the charcoal kilns. He rode only far enough to get out of sight of the pond, then cut back into the sparse forest to find another spot to tether his horse. On foot he worked his way to a spot fifty yards away from the pond where he couldn't be seen easily but had a decent enough view.

Slocum settled down, wishing he could build himself a cigarette but knowing the smoke would warn off his quarry. Instead, Slocum plucked a juicy stalk of grass and sucked at it. It was juicy but bitter and added to his mood. He wished Mira Van Winkle had not told him how her brother rode with the Mojave Guns. It complicated things immensely. He wanted to continue seeing her, but if Wilson caught any hint that Rafe Van Winkle was one of the outlaws, he'd reckon Slocum was giving Mira information about the silver shipments to pass along to her brother.

If he took in Rafe, Wilson would hang him. That wouldn't sit well with Mira. What girl's beau turned her brother over to a lynch mob? That cut Slocum's options down to about one, the way he saw it.

A half hour after settling in, Slocum heard horses picking their way through the trees. He slipped down and sat on the ground, using the broad bole of a pine to shield him from the two riders. As they went past, not ten feet away, he got a good look at them. Avery Caudell had to be the short, scrawny one with the nervous tic. As he rode it looked like his legs could hardly reach the stirrups, which had been pulled up as far as they'd go. Slocum reckoned the outlaw stood five feet tall, if that. But the other one had the same dark hair Mira sported. There was similarity, also, in the cheeks, but there the two went different paths. Rafe Van Winkle had a nasty scar across his face.

As he turned, Rafe showed that it was only one of many crisscrossing his face, which looked like a scarred checkerboard. His jaw was set and the hard look in his eyes belied what Mira had said of her brother. This was one determined owlhoot. Rafe Van Winkle might not be handy with the six-shooter hanging at his side, but Slocum had faced men who looked less dangerous and been surprised by their deadly behavior.

Was Mira trying to get him to underestimate her brother? Or did she truly believe he was an inept robber?

As silent as any Indian, Slocum moved closer to the pond so he could eavesdrop. He had to stop almost thirty

feet off, too far to hear clearly. Caudell remained on horseback between Slocum and the Van Winkles. Whatever was
being said, Mira was upset. She waved her arms around
and stomped her foot now and then. Rafe hung his head
like a guilty little boy, then looked his sister squarely in the
eye and answered. His words came clearer to Slocum.

". . . nobody's gonna tell me what to," Rafe Van Winkle
said.

"He's dangerous, Rafe!" his sister cried.

"I'm gonna ruin Wilson, that son of a bitch. He can't do
what he did and get away with it."

"You should tell Pa, if you won't tell me what your beef
with Wilson is," Mira said, her words uncertain.

"No!"

Rafe grabbed Mira by the shoulders and shook her, as if
trying to make her see reason. Slocum touched the butt of
his six-gun but did not draw. He didn't like the way Rafe
manhandled his sister, but revealing himself now might be
dangerous, for Mira and for himself. Caudell sat quietly,
pistol drawn, playing with his gun. Slocum would have to
shoot Caudell out of the saddle before dealing with Rafe
Van Winkle. The odds didn't look too good if he started
throwing lead, not with Mira likely to get in the line of fire.

Slocum faded back into the trees, went to his horse and
took off the lariat. He returned, saw that there weren't any
branches on the stunted pine trees low enough or strong
enough to suit his purpose. He spun the lariat a few times
and got the proper loop, then stood and waited.

Caudell and Rafe rode back within a few minutes, as he
had suspected when the argument with Mira had not gone
well. The two men argued as they came, distracting them
long enough for Slocum to step out, swing his lariat and
drop the loop around Caudell's thin shoulders. A strong
yank pulled the short man out of the saddle. Before he
could get his wind back from the fall, Caudell found himself hog-tied and helpless.

Slocum drew his six-shooter and pointed it straight at
Rafe Van Winkle.

"Don't get any funny ideas," Slocum said. "You can't draw faster 'n I can squeeze the trigger. And I don't miss."

"You're Slocum," Rafe said, his lip curling. Up close Slocum saw the pattern of scars was even more intricate than he'd suspected from a cursory glance. Such a spider web had not come about accidentally.

"And you're Rafe Van Winkle," Slocum said. "Now that introductions are out of the way, we've got a few things to discuss."

"Go on, shoot me. It's better 'n what Wilson would do to me." Rafe's hand moved to his cheek, tracing along the scars.

"Did Wilson do that to you?"

"You know he did. Mira's told you."

"What happened? You tell me," Slocum said. He kicked Caudell to keep him silent. The small man looked daggers at Slocum but kept quiet.

"He used a heated knife on my face. He should have driven it through my heart because I'm going to get even with him. I'll kill the son of a bitch, but not until after I've ruined him."

"Why'd he want to cut you up like that?" From what Slocum had seen of Wilson, he was a sharp businessman and had more than a touch of greed for the silver hidden in the mine, but he wasn't cruel.

"He . . . I know things about him. And he did it when I tried to kill him. I was only fourteen, but I swear I would have killed him."

"Your feud's with Wilson," Slocum said. "Not me. Not unless you try stealing the silver when I try to transport it for him. I take my job seriously."

"You're working for a bastard, Slocum!"

"Why? What'd he do to get you riled up?"

"I'm not gonna tell you and you can't sweet-talk it out of Mira when you're screwin' her because she doesn't know everything."

"My six-gun's got a hair trigger on it. Right now hearing you say things like that about your sister makes my finger twitch. You don't want that." Slocum kicked Caudell again to keep him from wiggling away.

"That's just fine. Mira doesn't know the half of it."

"You tell me."

"Go to hell. You're Wilson's toady."

"I work for him. I'm nobody's lickspittle," Slocum said in a cold voice.

"Are you going to shoot me or bore me to death with your lies?"

Rafe's defiance almost convinced Slocum to take him and Avery Caudell to Wilson, but something warned him against doing this.

"What's your beef with Wilson?"

"Ask Luther. Him and Wilson are inseparable."

"Luther's dead," Slocum said. "I killed him." The expression on Rafe's face puzzled Slocum even more. There was a flash of irritation, then complete anger.

"I wanted to kill him. Are you lying or did you really kill him?"

"He slugged me, robbed me and left me for dead out in the middle of Mahogany Flat. Luther wasn't too bright or he would have made sure I was dead before driving off."

"Then you *know* Wilson's a no-account snake," Rafe said. "Luther never did anything without being told by Wilson. If he tried to kill you, bet your bottom dollar it was because Wilson ordered him to do it."

"That doesn't make any sense. If Wilson wanted to get rid of me, all he'd have to do is fire me."

"Whatever he does, he has his reasons. They're likely to be crooked ones, too. Look at what he tried to do with all them mining deeds, him and George Hearst. If you're telling the truth, Slocum, you'd better watch your back. Or join us."

"The Mojave Guns?"

"We're not such a bad bunch," Rafe said. "You're not lily-white yourself. Nobody who swings a gun like you has a clean record."

"Got a clear conscience," Slocum said. "That's better. I never killed anybody who didn't deserve it."

"Don't you go killin' Pete Wilson! He's mine!"

Such powerful hatred built over the years. If Rafe told the truth and Wilson had given him the scars, he had been festering for more than ten years.

"Whatever's between you two is your business. If you try to take the silver, it becomes mine."

"You're letting me go?" Rafe's eyebrows rose, pulling the scars on his cheeks into a new and different pattern that was no less ugly than before.

"I've told you where I stand."

"And you better watch your back from up there, Slocum. If Luther didn't get you, another of Wilson's henchmen will. I don't know why he wants you dead, but that's the way you'll end up. Mark my words."

Slocum kicked Caudell again, then reached down and flipped the rope around freeing the man. Caudell swarmed to his feet and glared at Slocum. There was at least a foot difference in height. Slocum had seen pure venom in a man's gaze before and recognized it instantly now. He didn't know if Rafe was right about turning his back on Big Pete Wilson, but Slocum knew better than to give Avery Caudell any chance to shoot him in the back.

Caudell hissed like a snake, grabbed his saddle horn and clumsily pulled himself up into the saddle. His bowlegs wrapped around the horse, and he cruelly used his spurs to get the horse galloping off. As he made his way through the trees, he shot a look back at Slocum that reinforced the notion that there would be blood spilled between them.

Rafe Van Winkle hesitated, as if weighing Slocum's honesty. He shook his head, apparently unable to come to a conclusion and silently followed his partner through the pines. In seconds both outlaws were gone, leaving Slocum behind with a powerful lot of unanswered questions and more than a little doubt about his employer.

He shook his head, coiled his rope and returned to his horse for the ride back to the Silver Emperor Mine.

9

Slocum sat on a low hill overlooking the Silver Emperor Mine, waiting for sundown to ride back into camp. He watched the bustle of the miners as they went about their work, the antlike stream going in and out of the mouth of the mine, the sudden windstorm of dust rushing out as they blasted, the hurry to get in to pick out the best hunks of silver-laden ore. In the midst of it all Big Pete Wilson walked around, barking orders and making sure everything ran smoothly.

It was hard to think the man was capable of inflicting such scars on Rafe Van Winkle, but the young outlaw obviously believed it was true. And something else, more than the disfigurement, drove Rafe in his hatred of Wilson. One thing Rafe had said that worried at Slocum like a nettle under a saddle blanket.

Luther had worked for Wilson for a long time. Had the mine owner told the big dumb galoot to slug Slocum and leave him for dead in the middle of the desert? What reason could there be? If anything, Slocum had saved Wilson a pile of money by preventing the silver shipment from being stolen by the Mojave Guns. He should have been given a bonus, not a death sentence.

Slocum knew enough of the day-to-day workings of a mine to know everything at the Silver Emperor looked legit. As the sun sank low behind him, he stood, dusted himself off and started to mount when he saw Wilson accepting a shipment of silver ingots from the smelter. Something told him to watch a few minutes longer, and he was glad that he did. Wilson personally accepted the crates holding the silver, but he didn't call over men to load the freshly smelted silver onto the wagon. Curious at the way Wilson looked around, Slocum took out his binoculars and focused them on the mine owner. His behavior was even stranger when seen up close.

Grunting and struggling, he moved the crates himself a few yards away and covered them with a tarp. He placed large rocks on the corners of the tarp to keep it from flapping and only then did he call to a trio of miners to come over. When they got to where he stood, he pointed to a different stack of crates to load into the silver wagon.

Because of the way the mountain curved at the point near Wilson's shack to form a small box canyon, no one in the camp had seen his few minutes of effort dragging the hundred-pound crates away. And what was in the stack that got loaded? More silver? Why not try to ship it all rather than rely on hiding the newly smelted metal under a tarp? Slocum scratched his head, trying to figure it out.

He replaced his field glasses and walked down the hill and into the camp, leading his horse. He was in no hurry to return and needed time to think, but during the twenty minutes it took to return to the bunkhouse Slocum had no idea what to believe. Rafe Van Winkle? The man had hinted at dire things without saying anything definite. But the warning that Wilson had sent Luther to kill him had bothered Slocum because he saw a kernel of truth in it.

If not truth, then possibility. But why?

"Hey, Slocum you're back real early now. What's wrong? Your little filly kick you out?" The big miner's name was Herkimer and he had a slight British accent. Several others had gathered about, all of them smiling. Slocum knew they were all a mite jealous of him and Mira.

"Wore her out," Slocum said, swinging his gear around

to store it. His horse was in the corral avidly drinking from the trough. He'd go feed the horse later, after he had some victuals of his own. "She ended up crying for mercy. Being the considerate man that I am, I decided to give her the night off to recover."

This produced a round of laughter. Several of the men slapped Slocum on the shoulder, then handed him small flasks with their personal stash of rotgut. He accepted one or two swigs, mostly to make it appear he'd joined in the festivities.

"We're makin' right good progress in the mine," Herkimer told him. "Blasted today and got nuggets o' silver as bloody big as me fist."

"Too bad they ain't as big as your head," joked another. "It'd take two men to carry 'em out of the mine then!"

Slocum let the joshing ebb and flow through the bunkhouse, then excused himself to tend his horse. It took only a few minutes to feed and curry the animal, then Slocum's curiosity carried him upslope a ways and onto the path leading to Wilson's shack. But he wasn't hunting for the mine owner. He was more interested in the crates behind the shack.

He might have been in the sun too long or seen something wrong. The desert could play tricks on a man's eyes and mind. Slocum waited a few minutes to see if Wilson was going to poke his head out. When he didn't Slocum edged around back to the tarpaulin and stood staring at it. His heart beat a little faster. He didn't have any good reason but curiosity to be here poking into what wasn't any of his business.

He picked up the edge of the tarp and looked under it. The crates were marked with numbers like those on the silver shipments. Slocum took a deep breath, dropped to his knees and began prying free the lid of one crate. Without a pry bar it took longer than it should have, but once the nails had given a little bit, Slocum got his fingers under the lid and lifted. The screeching sound filled the quiet night.

Freezing, he waited to see if Wilson came boiling from

the shack to see what was making such a loud sound. No sign of the owner emboldened Slocum. He lifted the lid off all the way and reached into the crate. His fingers stroked over the cool, hard, slick sides of silver ingots. For a fleeting moment the idea of making off with a box or two of the unguarded silver flashed through his head. Then he pushed it away. He had a job—guarding this very silver.

It took several minutes longer to replace the lid and make sure it was properly nailed down, but Slocum took the time, using the butt of his pistol as a hammer. The last thing in the world Slocum wanted was for Wilson to suspect anyone had meddled with the crates.

Walking quickly back to the bunkhouse, he rounded the corner in time to see the wagon rattling down the road leading to Panamint City.

"Hey, wait!" he called, waving. The driver and guard couldn't hear him over the clatter made by the steel-rimmed wheels against the rocks in the road. Even the braying mules conspired to muffle his outcry.

"What's wrong, Slocum?"

"Mr. Wilson," Slocum said, seeing the owner come from the direction of the mine. "Where're they going with the wagon?"

"Don't worry your head none about that. I gave you the day off. You're still on vacation 'til tomorrow morning."

"But the wagon!"

"I had to get another silver shipment to Panamint City right away. You're the best I have, but Bustamante and Yarrow are good men. They'll see the silver safely to the bank vault."

Slocum half turned, then stopped himself. He had almost looked back toward Wilson's shack and the mountain of precious metal behind it.

"Where'd the silver come from?" Slocum asked.

"Freshly smelted this afternoon. Four crates' worth. What's wrong, Slocum? You look upset."

"The silver just come out of the smelter and you sent it off?"

"Straightaway to the banker," Wilson said. "By shipping it at night like this, I think we can avoid those bandits so intent on turning me into a pauper."

"I ought to go, to make sure nothing happens."

"Slocum, you need to learn to relax. Come on up to my place and have a drink. I've got a bottle of that champagne left over." Wilson chuckled indulgently. "I admit it. I took a couple bottles of the men's bubbly for my own use."

"I saw riders this afternoon. They might have been in the gang," Slocum said.

"You don't know that. You didn't talk to them, now did you? Come on, Slocum. Let's discuss business. If you're going to be foreman of this here mine, you need to be perfectly clear on what I expect from you." Wilson put his arm around Slocum's shoulders and steered him up the hill to his shack where they spent the next hour finishing off the champagne.

Wilson was a bit tipsy when Slocum left, but the cold night air sobered Slocum in a hurry. Rather than return to the bunkhouse, he saddled his horse and got on the road for Panamint City. He was hardly thirty minutes out when he ran into the wagon making its way back to the mine.

"What happened?" Slocum called.

"Robbed," gasped out Bustamante. "Not an hour back. Me and Yarrow we couldn't stop them. There was too many of them, and they got the drop on us. We didn't have a chance."

"They took the silver?"

"Sí, yes, that's what they did," said Bustamante. "They made us push out the crates and then chased us off."

"You get a look at their faces?"

"They wore masks, and it was darker 'n a whore's heart," said Yarrow. "But when one of them rode past, not more 'n the distance 'tween me and you, Slocum, I saw something."

Slocum turned to the still-frightened man and stared at

him, willing him to get on with it. Anything he knew could be important.

"Scars," Yarrow said. "He had a whole mess o' scars right above his mask. Here and here," Yarrow said, pointing to a spot high on his cheek and just under his eye.

About where Rafe Van Winkle's scars puckered his skin.

"Dark hair?"

"The robber? I don't know. It was dark, but he coulda had dark hair. You know him, Slocum?"

"No, but I will get to know him real intimate-like," Slocum said, tapping his six-shooter. Yarrow and Bustamante both swallowed hard. It was bad enough being on the receiving end of a robbery. To have a hard case like Slocum after them would be worse.

"Good luck. It was maybe three, four miles back down the road toward Panamint City," Yarrow said. "You want me to tell the rest and get a few men for a posse?"

"I'll handle it. Don't want to waste time." Slocum put his heels to his horse's flanks and rocketed off. As soon as he was out of sight, he slowed the pace and then let his horse walk. Exhausting the horse before he even found the road agents was foolish since he might have to chase the robbers halfway across Death Valley before he caught them.

"The Mojave Guns," he scoffed. He guessed Avery Caudell had ridden alongside Rafe, with several others from the gang to help out. Slocum had no qualms about going up against a half dozen of them. Caudell would be a handful when their paths crossed again because the little man had been so badly humiliated, and the others would be inclined to shoot Slocum out of hand. Rafe Van Winkle was probably in that camp, too. But Slocum thought very little of their skill as road agents. He wondered why Big Pete Wilson hadn't gotten together a decent posse and flushed them out long before now. With Zeb and Bennie dead, that ought to give more than enough incentive to bring the Mojave Guns to justice.

Instead, Wilson sent out a poorly-guarded wagon after dark as if begging the outlaws to rob it. And what had been in the crates that had rattled behind Yarrow and Bustamante? The silver from the smelter was still hidden behind Wilson's shack up in the hills.

Slocum rode more slowly when he reached the stretch of road where he thought the ambush had occurred. Going off the road afforded him a good view of the terrain. Even the meanest greenhorn would have to lie in wait behind a couple huge boulders that hid them from any traffic along the road. Jumping to the ground, Slocum quickly found that the Mojave Guns had picked this very spot for their attack. The remnants of more than one cigarette showed they had waited a considerable time.

He tried to make out how many there had been. At least four and possibly five, though there might have been one or two more. Walking around the rocks, he stood in the middle of the road looking back toward the Silver Emperor Mine, imagining what the scene had been like earlier.

Bustamante had driven straight into the ambush because Yarrow hadn't been suspicious enough to question the likelihood of outlaws lying in wait for them here. Slocum couldn't put too much blame on the young guard's shoulders. He had never ridden shotgun before, not that Slocum knew, and was looking down the barrels of as many as six pistols before he knew what was happening.

Slocum circled the area where the robbery had occurred and filled in details Yarrow and Bustamante had neglected—or simply never noticed. Two of the gang had kept them occupied looking forward while the rest went to the rear of the wagon and pulled out the crates. The heavy indentations in the roadbed showed where the crates had fallen. The outlaws had chased the two miners away toward Panamint City. Somewhere farther down the road they had turned around and returned to the Silver Emperor camp.

Slocum wasn't as interested in that as he was concerned about where the outlaws had taken the crates. He reckoned

four men had carried the silver crates down into a nearby
arroyo, two to each crate. Slipping and sliding, he got
down the steep embankment to the sandy bottom.

He felt no sense of accomplishment when he saw four
crates lying broken open beneath a tall, waxy-leafed creosote bush. Pausing, cocking his head to one side to listen
for any sound that might betray the presence of the outlaws,
Slocum waited until he heard a distant coyote howling
mournfully. A rabbit scampered about and jumped over the
crates on its way back to its burrow. This act of rabbit defiance convinced Slocum the road agents were long gone. He
still approached cautiously and stopped a few feet away.

Slocum frowned at what he saw. The heavy shadows
might have confused him but closer examination proved
this wasn't so. He dropped to his knees and pawed through
the contents of each of the four crates.

"Rocks. Nothing but tailings from the mine."

Slocum brushed off his hands and backed away, looking
around. This didn't make any sense. Why was Wilson
sending out two tenderfoot guards to protect a valuable
shipment—when the shipment was nothing but drossy
rock? The chance of Bustamante and Yarrow being robbed
was high, no matter what time they left. There was only
one road out of Wildrose Canyon going to Panamint City.
All it took was a solitary lookout to spot movement and re-
lay it to the rest of the gang, day or night. Firepower, not
stealth, would get the silver delivered safely.

Bustamante and Yarrow had been sent out with a load of
worthless rock. Wilson had risked their lives for what? It
didn't make any sense. Slocum checked the boxes again, to
make sure he hadn't jumped to some conclusion. The contents were definitely rock left after smelting. It wasn't even
ore with some silver content. Although it was a wild flight
of fancy, Slocum thought Wilson might have sent boxes of
ore to be assayed.

But he hadn't said that. He had claimed these were
crates of silver bars. Unless Bustamante and Yarrow had
been mistaken.

Slocum retraced his steps to the road, went around the rock and mounted his horse. The Mojave Guns hadn't been well rewarded for their daring this night.

"Rocks, just rocks," he muttered. As he started to circle the boulders and get back to the road, he heard hoofbeats approaching. Fast.

Slocum slipped his six-shooter from its holster and laid it low across his lap, waiting to see who was in such a powerful hurry in the middle of the night.

The rider shot past, then stood in the stirrups and pulled back hard on the reins. A dust cloud was kicked up, partially obscuring the ride.

Slocum stayed where he was and shifted the six-gun around to cover the rider.

"Slocum?"

"What are you doing out here, Mr. Wilson?" Slocum kept his pistol drawn but held it at his side as he rode forward. The mine owner was covered in dust and had a wild look about him.

"I came after you when Bustamante told me what had happened. You danged fool! You shouldn't ride out alone like that. You might get yourself killed. Those outlaws are dangerous!"

"Reckon they are," Slocum said. "They made off with four crates of silver bars."

"This the spot where they held up my wagon?" Wilson looked around. "It's a good spot. The Mojave Guns have used it before."

"Did Yarrow know that?"

"I might have told him," Wilson said. "He was as eager as a puppy dog to ride along. Don't know how much of what I told him that he listened to."

"Not much," Slocum said. He rode forward a few more strides, slipping his six-shooter back into his holster. "I made out at least four and probably six road agents lying in wait here. Two stopped the wagon, the other four unloaded the crates."

"They took them?"

Slocum heard the anxiety in Wilson's question. He was worried that the crates were still around with the evidence of nothing but drossy rocks inside.

"Reckon they did," Slocum said. "There's no easy way to carry that much silver without keeping it in a crate, is there?" He gave Wilson the chance to contradict him, to tell him this was some elaborate setup to lure out the Mojave Guns. But the trap had been piss-poor. If Wilson wanted to find the outlaws' camp, he ought to have had several men riding parallel to the road, ready to track the road agents when they took their plunder. Even an expert tracker like Slocum couldn't reliably follow a trail through the sunbaked alkali flats that made up so much of Death Valley.

"You figure they slung it on mules and got it out of here that way?"

"They might have done it that way," Slocum said slowly. "If they intended to head off the road, they wouldn't bother stealing the wagon. It wouldn't go a hundred yards in these rocks." That wasn't true, but he wanted to give Wilson some rope and see if the man knotted it around his neck.

He did.

"So they made off with four crates of silver. Damnation!" Wilson slapped his thigh and sent a cloud of dust rising. "I'm out four crates of silver worth eight thousand dollars or more! The damned thieves! I'll offer a reward! I'll see them all in hell for this!"

"Want me to track them? It'd be mighty hard, especially at night, but I might find their camp." Slocum tried to see the mine owner's face but couldn't in the dark.

"No, no, it was bad enough risking Yarrow and Bustamante. I don't know what I was thinking. I thought they could sneak past and get the silver to the bank. Damn, I hate it when I'm that wrong. I don't want any more risks taken like that. No, sir. Especially not you, Slocum. I need a good, strong hand at the mine."

"I'm a sight better at tracking. Give me a posse of ten

men, and I'll flush them out, no matter where they went to ground." He saw the rigidity in Wilson's shoulders. This was the last thing in the world he wanted.

"We'll get on back to camp and discuss it there. You've been through almost as much as the driver and guard tonight. When you're tired, you make mistakes."

"It was mighty good of you to come riding out the way you did," Slocum said. He couldn't keep a touch of sarcasm from his voice, but Wilson didn't hear it.

"Nothing I wouldn't do for any of my men. Come on back, Slocum. We got a lot of plottin' 'n plannin' to do if we want to get future silver shipments through."

"A lot of thinking to do," Slocum agreed, trying to piece together Wilson's peculiar behavior. It didn't fit, and he wondered what it would take to make it all come together into a picture that made sense.

10

The ten kilns were lined up like soldiers standing at attention on a parade ground. Slocum rode upwind of them to avoid the smoke billowing from their rounded tops. A new batch of charcoal had been started and would be ready by the end of the week. Slocum looked around for any sign of Mira but didn't see her. Her father, Sebastian Van Winkle, worked alongside several of the men to stoke the furnaces. He had a florid face now gleaming with sweat from exertion in the hot sun and standing so near the smoky furnaces. Working with the determination of a man half his age, he kept up well.

Slocum considered riding past. Big Pete Wilson had told him to go scouting to find the Mojave Guns' camp with an eye toward forming a posse and catching the lot of the road agents in one big raid. Slocum wasn't sure that was what the mine owner really had in mind from the way he talked. And Slocum wondered if Wilson had any inkling that anyone else knew the silver shipment still rested under a tarp behind his shack. Probably not or he would have done more than set a man like Luther to kill him.

"Morning, Mr. Van Winkle," Slocum called. "You're working mighty hard. Why not let your crew do such hard chores?"

"I never thought I'd hear you say a thing like that,

Slocum." Sebastian wiped at his forehead with a grimy handkerchief that was almost black with soot. When he finished moping at the sweat, he had transferred most of it to his skin, making him look like an Indian all decked out in war paint. Slocum tried to find the family similarity between Sebastian Van Winkle and his son and couldn't do it. Sebastian was tall, gaunt to the point of emaciation with the look of tanned hide drawn taut over his skeleton. His eyes lacked the coldness—or the fire—of his son, and their level of energy—or anger—was also at odds.

"It's too hot for most folks," Slocum said.

" 'Only mad dogs and Englishmen go out in the noon-day sun,' " Van Winkle quoted, laughing. "That smelter your boss runs could use twice the charcoal we produce."

"You've got the ore from Hearst's mine to think about, too," Slocum said. The man was amiable enough, making Slocum wonder if he even knew his son was riding with the Mojave Guns.

"You lookin' for Mira? She's off somewhere in the hills hunting for more trees. We've 'bout chopped down the best around here and need to keep finding new stands. Won't be another year 'fore we run out of trees entirely. Don't know what we'll do then."

"Shut down, move on," Slocum said.

"Won't be the first time." Van Winkle wiped more sweat from his face and sank down in the dubious shade afforded by the end kiln. Standing a dozen feet away Slocum felt the heat radiating from it. The brick oven might afford shade from the sun but it had to be hotter 'n a five dollar whore close up. Van Winkle didn't seem to notice.

"Where'd you and Mira drift in from?"

"Here and there," Van Winkle said. He turned a little morose as memories flooded back. "After Claire was killed, we never had much of a home. Just wandered around 'til we ended up here."

"What happened? The flu? Cholera?" Slocum knew he was out of line asking but something made him want to find out.

"No," Van Winkle said. He clipped the word hard, short, ending discussion. "Claire died. That was 'bout the same time me and Mira lit out."

"You have a son, too, don't you?"

"Him?" Van Winkle snorted in disgust. "Don't know what happened to Rafe. 'Til his ma died, he was a good boy. Then he got right moody and eventually never came home. That's when me and Mira moved south."

"You were up north?"

Sebastian Van Winkle nodded.

"You never heard from Rafe again?"

"What's your interest in him, Slocum?"

"Not much. Just that Mira mentioned him a time or two, and I wondered."

"He's gone as sure as Claire. I don't know that he's in the ground pushin' up daisies somewhere, but he probably is. I got to get back to work. Why don't you ride on back come sundown? Mira'll be here then."

"Thanks," Slocum said, not intending to do any such thing. He had a good idea where Mira would go scouting for more timber. Riding from the line of kilns back in the direction of the Silver Emperor, he cut off the road when he got out of sight and rode directly into the hills forming Wildrose Canyon. Telescope Peak to the south drew him, but he thought Mira's attention would be in a different section of the Argus Mountains. Within a mile he found fresh spoor and within two he knew he was on the woman's trail. Her pony had a nicked shoe that left a distinctive print whenever it crossed soft earth.

The wooded area turned into a sparse forest and then became denser as Slocum continued up the side of the mountain. When he saw a second set of tracks alongside Mira's he knew he had figured out what was going on. He cut off at an angle, in case Rafe Van Winkle kept watch on his back trail, then circled so he'd come up on brother and sister from a direction they weren't likely to be paying much attention to.

Slocum dropped to the ground when he heard voices.

Advancing on foot, he peered out at Mira and Rafe. She had a scrap of paper clutched in her hand and a pencil stuck behind her ear. Slocum reckoned she might have been scouting for new trees to turn into charcoal when her brother found her. More likely, they had agreed to meet here.

"I don't care," she said angrily. "You can't keep on doing this."

"You don't understand," Rafe said. "I'd kill the son of a bitch—"

"Rafe! Don't swear!"

"You ain't our ma," the man said, his anger unabated. "I'd kill that son of a bitch Wilson, but I want to make him squirm first. The best way to do that's to steal his most precious possession."

"His silver," Mira said in a small voice. "What will you do when you and those terrible men you're riding with completely loot all of his silver?"

"I'm going to kill him as slow and painful as I can. I want him to suffer."

"Why do you hate him so, Rafe? What's he ever done to you?"

Slocum listened more intently now. Rafe had accused Wilson of giving him the scars on his face. Didn't Mira know that or had Rafe lied to him about it?

The small move Rafe made, hand starting for his face and then being checked, told Slocum what the truth was. Big Pete Wilson had cut up Rafe's face something fierce, but why hadn't he ever told his sister?

"There're some things you're better off not knowing," Rafe said.

"Because I'm a girl? Because I'm younger than you? Because I'm not tough enough?" Mira stepped forward and let fly with a punch that ended in Rafe's belly. He gasped, doubled and turned slightly to cover the full effect of the blow. Rafe ended up facing Slocum but not seeing much. His eyes were clamped shut, and his scars had turned a bright pink.

Slocum grinned in appreciation. Mira Nell Van Winkle was no hothouse flower. She could take care of herself, and it was high time her brother figured that out.

"Believe me when I say you don't want to know." Rafe straightened and rubbed his belly. "That's quite a punch you've got there."

Mira made another fist and waved it under his nose.

"Tell me your beef with Wilson. Tell me or you'll get another dose of this!"

Rafe backed off far enough so she couldn't carry out her threat.

"I'm not sayin' another word," Rafe said. "What he did was terrible. And if I told you, you'd tell Pa."

"Pa? What's he got to do with you hating Mr. Wilson?"

"You listen for once in your life," Rafe said. "You and Pa clear out. You don't want to be anywhere around when I settle accounts with Wilson. It's taken me years to track him down, and I don't want you around to foul things up."

"Pa's as bullheaded as you are," Mira said. "He'd never listen to a thing I said. You tell him. Go on, I dare you! You ride on down to the kilns and you tell him. You haven't talked to him since . . . since you lit out and left us."

Again Slocum saw Rafe make an abortive move to touch the scars on his face.

"You can't keep it a secret forever, Rafe. Not 'less you turn to smoke and blow away on the wind again."

"I'm not going to do any such thing. I'm making my stand. I'm not cutting and running as long as Wilson is breathing the same air. He's going to die, Mira, he's going to die by my hand!"

"Oh, you!" Mira stamped her foot, spun and stalked off. Slocum watched her mount and ride away without another word. Her chin thrust up in the air, she rode stiffly, her irritation obvious in every bone of her body, every gesture she made, even the very radiance she gave off.

"Don't you go tellin' Pa we've been talkin'!" Rafe shouted after her. "No good will come of it, if you do!"

Rafe Van Winkle picked up a rock and heaved it into the

trees as hard as he could. When the rock hit a tree trunk it sounded like a ricocheting bullet. He kicked at another rock like a willful child, then went to mount. Slocum stepped from the trees and advanced a few paces. Rafe froze, knowing instantly he was not alone even though Slocum had not made a sound or called the outlaw out.

"Go for that pistol on your hip and I'll cut you down where you stand," Slocum said when it was apparent Rafe was going to turn and throw down.

"What do you want? You fixin' on takin' me to Wilson for the reward? I know he's got a reward out."

"He probably does, but I'm not a bounty hunter," Slocum said. The notion of being a bounty hunter didn't sit well with him.

"You take his pay, you eat his food, you sleep in his bunkhouse. Is all that enough to kill a man, Slocum?"

"I've killed men for less."

"So you'll shoot me in the back?"

"Never done that," Slocum said. "I'm not going to start with you."

"So you're going to talk me to death?"

"I intend to give you some advice that'll keep you alive. I don't know what your feud is with Wilson, but it ends here and now. You keep riding with the Mojave Guns and I'll see you hanged."

Rafe Van Winkle laughed harshly. "I don't scare off that easy, Slocum. And I've got a big feud with Wilson that you're not going to argue me out of."

"What is it? Why'd he cut you up the way he did?"

"I found him—" Rafe bit back the rest of his words. Slocum saw how the young man shook with rage and knew he would explode.

"If I ask Wilson, you reckon he'd tell me?"

"He thinks I'm dead."

"Is that it? You two mixed it up, he sliced your face and thought you were dead. Now you're coming to get revenge on him?"

"There's more."

Again Slocum heard the ring of truth in Rafe's words. He also heard the iron determination not to speak further. Whatever the reason he plotted revenge on Big Pete Wilson, it went beyond having his face cut up. And neither Sebastian Van Winkle nor Mira knew the actual reason. Rafe played it close to the vest.

Too close for Slocum's taste.

"What's it going to be? You ride on out of here. Go back north, maybe, where you came from."

Slocum hadn't expected the sudden eruption of motion at that suggestion. Rafe went into a crouch as he spun, his hand flashing to his six-shooter. Slocum was a fraction of a second slow, but he didn't have to turn. He whipped up his Colt Navy and fanned three quick rounds.

Rafe grunted, then got off a shot of his own that took off Slocum's hat. He recoiled as the hat whipped away, the drawstring catching his ear and distracting him. By the time he got his six-gun back in line, Rafe had taken cover.

"I didn't mean for it to be this way, Rafe."

"Why not? You're sweet on my sister. You work for Wilson. You kill me and everything'll fall into your lap. You get a big, fat reward *and* Mira."

"If I'd wanted to gun you down, I could have done it any time."

"Yeah, sure, you wanted to give me a break. A chance to act like a yellow-bellied coward and run!"

Slocum moved slowly to get a better view of the gully where Rafe had taken refuge. He realized the man was only taunting him to draw him out. He had fired three times, and Rafe had shot only once. The battle seemed to be in the outlaw's favor, but Slocum only needed one clean shot to end it. He was a better marksman and both of them knew it.

"I don't want to kill you. It'd be too damn hard to explain to Mira," Slocum said, circling, trying to flush Rafe. As he came to a spot where he looked down into the gully, he cursed. Rafe had vanished into thin air.

Reacting more by instinct than because of anything he

had seen or heard, Slocum dived forward, rolled down the side of the ravine and fetched up hard at the bottom. Bullets sang through the space Slocum had vacated so abruptly. Finding their positions reversed, Slocum looked up and saw Rafe's hat poking up over the edge.

Slocum didn't fire. Instead he faked a loud moan, then cut it off with a gasp. He balanced his pistol carefully against a rock to steady it for a more accurate shot, waiting, waiting, waiting.

The hat never moved. After a few seconds, Slocum knew that Rafe wasn't falling for his trick any more than he had for Rafe's attempt to draw his fire and make him waste more ammo.

Slocum made his way uphill, stumbling on fist-sized rocks under his boots, until he found a narrow crevice. Knowing that he might be making a prime target of himself but seeing no way around taking the risk, he forced himself between the rocks, spotting small, bright scratch marks showing that Rafe had preceded him this way. In spite of himself, Slocum grudgingly admired Rafe's quick thinking and fast action to avoid what might have been a deadly trap. Slocum popped out on the other side of the fissure, getting a good view of the spot where Rafe had thrust a stick into the ground and then placed his hat on it. Wind blew through the forest and caused the hat to bob about, but of the hat's owner there wasn't a trace.

Waiting, listening, Slocum figured Rafe would make a mistake. But the young man was smarter than that. When he had failed to draw Slocum's fire with his hat, he had hightailed it. Slocum took another few minutes to come to the conclusion Rafe wasn't simply trying to draw him out again.

In disgust he walked to the hat and grabbed it. Slocum turned in a full circle, but Rafe was nowhere to be seen. Stomping back to where his own hat lay, Slocum picked it up and settled it on his head. He wasn't sure what to do with Rafe's hat, but he wasn't going to simply leave it.

Slocum mounted and headed back to the Silver Emperor Mine, fuming at his failure to stop Rafe Van Winkle.

11

"You out there takin' trophies now, Slocum?" Herkimer pointed to Rafe's hat slung over the saddle horn. The miner came closer and looked up, squinted at the sun, moved a bit more and let the light pouring through the hole in the brim of Slocum's hat fall on his face. "You might bloody well deserve some kinda trophy, eh?"

"Found it," Slocum said. "I'll return it when I find its owner."

"Yeah, sure, whatever you say, Slocum," said Herkimer.

"What's wrong?" Slocum looked around the Silver Emperor camp and felt a tension that hadn't been there when he'd ridden out. It took him another couple seconds to realize what bothered him most. The miners weren't in the mine drilling rock and moving ore out to be separated and graded before being sent to the smelter. Instead, they milled about the mouth of the mine. "You have a cave-in? Damp?"

Slocum knew these were dangers miners feared most. The timbers supporting the roof of the shaft were green, weak, left over after the charcoal kilns had already swallowed the best seasoned wood into their voracious maws. And damp—gas—could kill dozens of men before anyone noticed. More than one miner had driven a pickax through a rock, hit a pocket of methane and set off an explosion.

But the slow leaking of the gas was more to be feared. Slocum didn't remember seeing any of the miners carry a canary or other small bird into the shaft to use as a detector for the dangerous fumes.

"Nuthin' like that," Herkimer said. "We got to talkin'."

Slocum tensed. It was never good when a miner said something like that. Rumors flew like high-soaring birds when miners "got to talkin'." From such "talkin'" could come all manner of trouble.

"What's the problem, then?"

"Well, Slocum, see, it's like this. We figure there's a powerful lot of silver bein' took from the mine. We're sweatin' in them hot tunnels. You ain't been all the way down to know what it's like when we hit water. It's boilin' hot. Well, we want more pay. We heard rumors that Wilson was gonna divvy up the extra silver as a bonus."

"Extra silver?"

"We was pullin' a goodly amount from the mine before we struck that new vein. Way we look at it, that new silver's nuthin' he had counted on to pay his bills. Why not split it 'twixt the lot of us strugglin' to get it out?"

Slocum remembered Luther's contention that the fewer men in the camp, the bigger the slice of the pie—the silver pie—there would be for him. It hadn't made much sense then and it still didn't. Wilson wasn't likely to do more than give a bonus. Actually cutting the miners in on the profits was unheard of. Slocum told Herkimer this.

"We didn't think you'd be with us on this, Slocum. You bein' management and all."

"Management?" For a moment, Slocum couldn't figure out what Herkimer meant. Then it hit him. Wilson had named him foreman, but that had been more of a tip of the hat in his direction for services rendered than an actual job. Since then he had spent more time over at the Modock Kilns than he had on-site at the Silver Emperor Mine, tracking down Rafe Van Winkle and trying to figure out what the hell was going on with the bogus silver shipments Wilson was making.

"We'd kinda hoped you would talk to him for us. You and him get along good."

"I'll see what I can do," Slocum said. His mind raced. Maybe Wilson was hoarding the silver to make it look as if the mine wasn't very profitable and he couldn't pay the miners more. That didn't make a whole lot of sense, but Slocum had a heap of digging to do before finding out what really went on at the Silver Emperor.

He trooped off to the shack where Wilson hung his hat and knocked on the door. He couldn't help straining a mite to look around to see if the tarp and the crates with the silver bars in them were still behind the shack. Slocum didn't get a chance to see for sure since the door opened. Wilson looked daggers at him.

"Well? What's the problem?"

"I tried to chase down one of the Mojave Guns. He got away," Slocum said. He saw how Wilson's eyes narrowed at the sight of the bullet hole in his hat brim. Slocum made no move to cover the hole or otherwise draw attention to it. "I need to know what you meant when you said I was foreman around here."

"Why, just that, Slocum. You can run things, keep them running. Watch over the shipments to Panamint City."

"Represent any gripes the men might have?"

Wilson heaved a deep sigh and stepped back. "Come on in. We got to talk this out, I see."

"Reckon so," Slocum said. He entered the cabin for the first time and was surprised at how nicely furnished it was for looking like nothing more than a line shack on the outside. The walls were covered with heavy newspaper to keep the wind and dust out, and the roof looked to have a foot or more of paper to insulate it from the treacherously hot desert sun. A window at the side of the cabin looked over the tarp and the crates beneath it; Slocum had to force himself not to stare or appear too curious.

The furniture was nicely crafted and the bed looked downright comfortable, unlike the thin pallets Slocum and the rest of the miners slept on over at the bunkhouses. Real china plates and flatware stood on a serving table to one side of the iron stove that furnished heat at night and cooking for meals. Slocum couldn't help noticing that Wilson fed charcoal from a large burlap bag rather than using wood in the stove.

"You want a drink? Don't have any more of that champagne but this might interest you." Wilson sat a quarter-filled whiskey bottle on the table and pointed to the chair across from him for Slocum.

"This is part of my problem, Mr. Wilson," Slocum said. "I don't know if I'm fish or fowl."

"What's that mean? You sayin' you're chicken?"

"If I'm actually foreman, I have a responsibility to the miners."

"You work for me. Just like them shirkers." Wilson poured two fingers of whiskey into a pair of shot glasses and pushed one across to Slocum. Wilson picked up his, eyed it with real appreciation, then downed it in a gulp. He belched, wiped his lips on his sleeve and set the glass back on the table. Slocum was slower to follow suit.

The whiskey was good and went down smooth to burn in the pit of his stomach. He licked the rim of the glass, wishing he could ask for more, but he had business to tend to. Business for the miners.

"They're looking for a cut of the new production from the mine," Slocum said. "Seems fair enough a request. They've worked their asses off and more than doubled the silver output, by my estimate."

"You're wrong. The road agents stole four crates of silver the other night. That's a flat-out loss that has to be made up."

"What do you mean *made up?* That sounds like you have a quota. You own the mine. How can you have a quota?" Slocum saw Wilson's lips thin as if he fought to hold back an angry outburst. The man poured himself another drink. This time he didn't offer Slocum one.

"You don't know what's going on here, Slocum. There's no way I can give the men a red cent more 'n they get now. I can't. Things have changed and not for the better."

"It's mighty hard for them to see that, after you gave them champagne and congratulated them on finding the new vein of ore."

"Nothing more. If you can't get them back to work, I'll fire the lot of them."

"You won't get any silver from the mine if you do that," Slocum pointed out.

"Panamint City's got dozens of layabouts who'd come to work here for half of what I pay those sluggards!"

"I'll talk to them, but they won't like it."

"Then fire them!"

"That's your job," Slocum said flatly. He got to his feet, then hesitated. He was missing something else with Big Pete Wilson. Then he remembered Luther. How many others among the miners were beholden to Wilson and Wilson alone? "You have anyone who can back me up?" Slocum asked suddenly. This caught Wilson by surprise.

The mine owner had nodded once by the time he caught himself.

"Get out there, Slocum. Do your job."

Slocum walked outside, knowing what it felt like to mount a gallows, the noose in plain view. He stood on a small hill of tailings and looked out over the crowd of a hundred miners, feeling very alone. They milled about, muttering among themselves until Herkimer shouted for them to be quiet so Slocum could talk.

"The word's not good," Slocum said, and he realized right away that wasn't the way to start. He wasn't going to sugarcoat the news, though. That wasn't his way. "Wilson won't give you any bonus, and when I asked him to give you all raises, he turned that down, too."

"Kill him!" shouted someone in the rear of the crowd. Slocum wondered who the man meant or if it mattered. The miners were angry, and anyone would do to rip apart.

"Wait!" Slocum held up his hand and a few of the closer miners fell silent while others toward the rear of the crowd continued to grumble. "If you go on strike, you might get him to give you a raise."

"We're only gettin' a dollar a day and *he's* gettin' rich!"

The miner who had spoken cut off his words suddenly when the man next to him swung his elbow and caught him smack in the mouth. Spitting blood and teeth, the first miner laid into his attacker, whaling the tar out of him. This set off a fight throughout the crowd. Slocum stood and watched helplessly. To step between any of those battling miners would be instant death. They were angry and needed to vent some steam. Slocum wished they weren't taking it out on each other, but since they were, he was going to step back and let them have at anybody dumb enough to come within swinging distance.

When one miner took a swing at Slocum, he ducked and shoved with all his might, sending the man stumbling back into the crowd where he quickly found others to fight.

Slocum's hand went to his six-shooter when Herkimer struggled up the rise to join him.

"Ain't no call to put a bullet in me," Herkimer said. "No way to stop 'em. I seen this happen before, and it's gonna get even uglier."

"You see what I do?" Slocum asked.

Herkimer nodded glumly. "Them's Wilson's henchmen out there keepin' the fight goin'."

"Luther was one of his boys, wasn't he?"

"Surely was. So's that one and him and him," Herkimer said, pointing out the men most intent on stirring up trouble. "Can't figure what he gains, settin' them against us like that."

Slocum shook his head. He didn't understand, either. It was as if Wilson wanted trouble at the mine. He was stealing silver and blaming it on the Mojave Guns, but how could he steal more if the miners weren't working?

"The ore's still high quality?" Slocum asked Herkimer.

"What? Oh, yeah, sure is. 'Bout the finest silver mine I've ever worked in and I seen some dandies in my day. Ever' day we ain't in there grubbin' out the carbonate, he's losin' money. Lots of it."

The fight was winding down, with no clear winners. The men Slocum identified as being Wilson's thugs had given as good as they got. More than a dozen men were on the ground, some barely moving. Doc Lonigan already made his way through, going from one fallen battler to the next. After pressing his palm down on one man's chest, Lonigan backed off, stood and came to the foot of the hill. He looked up at Slocum and Herkimer, glummer than he had ever looked.

"That one's dead, Slocum. Looks like he got his damn fool head beat in with something hard."

"What's going on?" demanded Wilson, bustling up. He had strapped on a six-gun and walked with his coat pulled away so he could grab the hogleg if he needed it. "Sweet Mother of Jesus!" he gasped, looking out over the crowd. Slocum thought the reaction was mighty false and that Wilson had taken his time showing up, as if waiting for the worst of the fight to be over before putting in an appearance.

"One's dead," Lonigan said. "The rest are pretty well beat up."

"Give us our fair share, Wilson!" shouted a miner, advancing on the owner. When the miner balled his hands into meaty fists, Wilson reached for his six-shooter.

"There's no call for that," Slocum called. Both Wilson and the miner jerked around to look at him, not sure which of them he spoke to.

"Which side you coming down on, Slocum?" demanded the miner. "With him or with us?"

"We're all on the same side in this," Slocum said.

"No, we're not," snapped Wilson. "I won't have any murderers on my payroll. You all clear out!"

"What?" bellowed the miner.

"You're fired. The lot of you are fired!"

Slocum drew and fired, his bullet kicking up dirt at the toes of the miner. The man glared up at Slocum, growled deep in his throat, then reconsidered his attack.

"You're as bad as he is, Slocum. Rot in hell!" With that, the miner spat and stormed off.

"Thanks, Slocum. You saved me having to shoot him," Wilson said.

"I didn't do it for you," Slocum said. "I did it to keep you from killing a good man." He felt Herkimer shift beside him. Slocum's arm shot out and blocked Herkimer's path to the mine owner.

"Glad to see you boys are still with me," Wilson said, misinterpreting what was going on. "Clear out the riffraff. They're all fired. But if they want a job, they can come see me one at a time, and I'll decide which to rehire."

"Who's going to work the mine?" asked Herkimer. "There's a powerful lot of folks out there who won't want to get rehired."

"And I don't want them. I'll go into town and see if anyone's interested in putting in an honest day's work for a decent wage." Wilson backed away, nodded in Slocum's direction and then almost ran toward his shack.

"Now don't that beat all," Herkimer said.

Slocum watched the ebb and flow of the fight as it died down. The miners knew what their boss—their former boss—had said. Most were already on their way, some hobbling, others being helped by friends, to the bunkhouses to gather their gear. The best of them were leaving and wouldn't have any trouble finding work at other mines in the Argus Mountains. And the ones remaining were the bully-boys Slocum thought were Wilson's private police force.

They made their way, not to the bunkhouses, but to Wilson's shack to be "rehired."

"Where do you stand?" Slocum asked Herkimer. "You got put onto Wilson's side, somehow."

"I reckon I'll stand 'bout where you do, Slocum. You got a good head on your shoulders and know more 'bout this mess than anybody else."

Slocum snorted in derision. He suspected a lot and knew nothing. But he appreciated Herkimer's support. He hoped it didn't cost the miner his life.

12

The silver coins weighed heavily in Slocum's pocket. He kept touching the hefty lump, as if it might grow feathers and fly away when he wasn't paying attention. He dropped heavily into the creaking chair at the back of the saloon situated smack in the center of Panamint City and looked around. It was just past noon, and he had driven the wagon in to pick up supplies—and to recruit workers. The specie in his pocket had been given to him by Wilson for that purpose. But the look of the men in the bar made Slocum wonder if he could find more than a pair of men in the entire area worth their pay.

Not that the pay Wilson was offering to miners amounted to much. He had slashed the·wages by half for newly hired miners. Herkimer and the others remaining, including Wilson's private army, continued to get their regular pay, but enticing new workers would be a problem. Slocum sat with a cool beer in his hand, thinking hard on the matter. He was certain Wilson had provoked the riot at the mine where so many had been hurt and one man killed. This had put such a bad taste in the mouths of most decent miners, they had packed their gear and had moved on before the sun set.

"Why?" Slocum wondered aloud.

"Why what, mister?" asked a pretty waiter girl. "How

much is a question I can answer. And the answer's four bits. And that's not four *bites*, either. That'll cost you extra. Plenty extra!" She laughed at her crude joke, bent over and shook her shoulders so other parts of her anatomy bounced and jiggled for Slocum's approval.

He looked up and hardly saw the shaking pulchritude. She straightened, looked outraged that she had failed to get an offer from him, and stalked off. Within minutes she and a grizzled old miner were at the bar talking like old friends.

Slocum was distracted by other, more perplexing matters. His mind refused to let loose of the questions tumbling about like a dust devil. Wilson was doing what he could to ruin a perfectly good claim. When Slocum had arrived a month earlier, the Silver Emperor had been run expertly and well. Only in the past week or so had Wilson turned squirrelly about the operation, doing things that made no sense. He was stealing his own shipments and making it appear that the Mojave Guns gang was responsible. There wasn't a marshal or sheriff within a hundred miles that cared to go after the road agents. But the silver was Wilson's. Why did he want it to appear that the gang was robbing him blind?

Slocum tried to figure out how Wilson might be in cahoots with the Mojave Guns, but the times he had talked to Rafe Van Winkle made it unlikely Wilson had anything to do with the outlaws. If Rafe had caught wind of it, he would have killed Wilson then and there.

That was another poser. What was Rafe's feud with Wilson? From the sound of it, Mira and her father had come to this part of the country fairly recently, as had Wilson. They did business, the kilns selling charcoal to Wilson's smelter, and nothing untoward had happened. From the way Mira talked, she rather liked Wilson and gave no indication of having known him before coming to Death Valley.

Slocum finished his beer and leaned back in the chair to give the saloon customers a once-over. He had thought coming to the saloon early in the afternoon might give him a step up on hiring those miners who were out of work.

From the look of the broke-down pissants around him, there was good reason they were out of work. He could count on the fingers of his hand the miners he would even consider shaking hands with. Others were out of work for obvious reasons. Some hobbled on gimpy legs, one had his arm in a sling and yet another needed help and was being led around by the hand because he wore fresh bandages over his eyes.

Slocum heaved to his feet and left the saloon. Stepping into the street was like being hit with a hammer. The noonday heat was rising rapidly and would be at its worst in another couple hours. Wiping a river of sweat off his forehead, Slocum went to the general store to place his order for the supplies needed at the mine. As he entered the cooler general store, the owner looked up. A quick appraisal of him and who he was generated a contemptuous snort.

"I need some supplies," Slocum said. "For the Silver Emperor."

"Reckoned so." The owner went back to reading his newspaper, San Francisco's *Alta California*, about a week old from the date Slocum read upside down.

"Too hot for you?"

"How's that?" This got the owner's attention.

"A customer comes in, aren't you supposed to jump to helping fill his order? Or has the heat boiled your brains?"

"Don't go gettin' snotty on me, boy," the owner said. He was hardly older than Slocum but had the attitude of a man twice his age. Something was causing the superior attitude, and Slocum wanted to find out what it was. He reached over and grabbed the man by the front of his apron and lifted. The owner staggered back a step, then fetched up against the counter.

"You're the one who needs a lesson in manners."

"You don't scare me," the owner said bravely enough, but Slocum read the fear on his face.

"No need to be afraid, if you fill my order." Slocum released him. The owner scurried around the counter and looked intent on keeping it between them as long as possible.

"What do you want?"

"Got the list here," Slocum said, pulling it out of his shirt pocket and dropping it on the counter. The store owner made no move to touch it, as if it might grow fangs and bite him.

"You gonna pay up?"

"As always," Slocum said, only to be startled at the re-action. The man dived under the counter and pulled out a scattergun. Slocum leaned forward, pinned the barrel to the counter with one hand and grabbed the apron again with his other. "What's eating you?"

"You work at the Silver Emperor. I want my money 'fore you get another damn thing from this store."

"Mr. Wilson's run up a bill?" Slocum wasn't sure if this surprised him or not. Wilson had been acting increasingly strange. When Slocum had first ridden to Panamint City, all the mine's bills were paid. Somehow, finding that Wilson owed a considerable sum to the general store didn't seem out of the ordinary.

"Big one. Close to a hundred dollars."

The owner released the shotgun and pulled out a ledger book. He flipped it open and showed Slocum the bottom line on the "Silver Emperor" page, underlined twice in red.

"This'll go a ways toward paying the bill," Slocum said, fishing out stacks of the silver cartwheels he had been given to tempt new miners to come to work at the mine. He dropped a few pitiful additional coins on the counter to join the silver.

"Twenty dollars and a couple bits over," the store owner said, meticulously counting. "You still owe a passel."

"Fill what you can of that," Slocum said, his voice carrying an edge. "You'll get paid. My word on it."

"Your word," the owner scoffed. He reared back as Slocum grabbed for him again.

"My word's good."

"Sorry, sure it is, mister. I . . . I'll do what I can on the new order, but you gotta pay more promptly or I'm gonna cut you off. You tell Wilson that!"

Slocum stepped away, fuming mad. He left without another word, again entering the blast furnace of a Death Valley midday. On impulse, Slocum went to the bank. The instant he stepped into the lobby, two armed guards turned toward him, hands tightening on the rifles they held. He walked past them without so much as giving notice at their alertness and went to the bank president seated at his desk behind a low wood railing.

"I need a word with you, sir," Slocum said. The banker looked up, frowned, then motioned for Slocum to come around and sit in the fancy leather chair opposite the ornately carved desk.

"What can I do for you, Mr. Slocum?"

"I wondered if the loan Mr. Wilson asked about has been decided on." Slocum was taking a shot in the dark, and it got a mite murkier when the banker looked confused.

"I don't know what you're talking about, Mr. Slocum. Pete Wilson's not applied for any loan." The banker shook his head. "Fact is, he couldn't get one any more than you could."

"He's appointed me foreman of the Silver Emperor, so I figured you might be able to confide some of the business details."

"A foreman? Not to berate you or your ability, Mr. Slocum, but foremen are a dime a dozen in these parts. Don't know a single mine foreman who does anything more than herd the miners around. You need more than a title to be privy to financial matters."

"Even though I bring in the silver shipments?"

"Even then," the banker said. "Might I ask why you're inquiring?"

"Mr. Wilson needs to hire more miners and had talked about getting advances on their salaries."

"He's in no position to get a loan through *this* bank," the president said. "Tell him he's got another silver shipment due in San Francisco by the end of the month."

"To cover expenses there?"

The banker looked quizzically at Slocum, then shook

his head. "Just tell him, Mr. Slocum. He'll understand what is meant."

"Thanks," Slocum said, getting to his feet and wandering off more confused than before. If Wilson was strapped financially at the mine, coming to the bank where he deposited his silver shipments was the logical place to get a loan. But the banker had hinted that Wilson not only had not applied for any loan, but also that he could not. The flat-out statement about silver being due in San Francisco sounded more like an order than a suggestion. Something had gone wrong at the Silver Emperor Mine, and Slocum was at a loss to figure what it might be.

He shrugged it off and returned to the bar where he had begun his hunt for new miners. The sun was dipping lower now over the Panamint Mountains and the workers drifted in for a shot or two to kill the pain of their labors. Slocum staked a claim to a table and watched as the men came and went, sorting through them and finally deciding he didn't have the option of being choosey. He had to take what he could get.

Using what money he had left to buy four bottles of booze, he sat back at his table, a bottle in front of each empty chair. It took less than five minutes for the curious arrangement to draw men to find out what was going on.

"If you sit and drink, it means you want a job at the Silver Emperor Mine," Slocum explained. "The earlier you sign on, the more you get to drink."

There was a rush of men to get to the chairs, some pushing others out of the way. Slocum counted himself lucky at this selection process. The ones most easily discouraged from sitting and drinking were likely to be the ones least inclined to work. They certainly showed no initiative or spunk.

By the time the four bottles were drained, Slocum had nine mostly drunk new employees ready to make the trip back to the mine. Slocum herded them outside and got them into the wagon, which had been loaded with most of the supplies Wilson had sent him to town to purchase.

There'd be words exchanged about the bill at the general store when he got back, Slocum knew, but he didn't like being put in the position of guaranteeing payment. Even worse, he didn't like the store owner's attitude, as if the Silver Emperor Mine wasn't that important a customer any longer.

Slocum tried to ignore the drunken singing by the nine miners as they rattled and bounced back down the road through Wildrose Canyon to the mine, then joined them in their boisterous off-key renditions of songs none of them knew all that well.

"There's the bunkhouse, men," Slocum said, pointing. "Find yourselves an empty space and it's yours."

The men tumbled from the wagon, struggling to figure which bunkhouse Slocum had pointed out. It didn't matter, but Slocum wanted to keep the drunks together, at least for the night, to prevent them from disturbing the remaining miners. More than this, Slocum wanted to identify which of the miners still in camp were working directly for Wilson and against the interests of the others. The fight had shown clear lines Slocum wanted to maintain, for his own peace of mind as well as the safety of the newcomers. Wilson had his own private police force and crossing any of them spelled trouble.

Slocum went into the bunkhouse and counted heads. Less than a quarter of the bunks were filled. The nine newcomers would find themselves doing the work of two for quite a spell—and at half the wages the departed miners had received. This didn't sit well with Slocum, but little did anymore. Again the notion of leaving crossed his mind. Big Pete Wilson had given him the job when he was flat broke and so hungry his belly rubbed up against his backbone every time he moved, but that had been a month back.

A month ago, before he had met Mira. Using a woman as an excuse for staying at the Silver Emperor was a dumb idea, and Slocum knew it. But he felt some obligation to the men he had just hired, as well as more than a little curiosity about what was happening at the mine. He made

sure the drunk miners were all bunked out and left to find
Wilson and tell him about his newly hired first shift.

As he stepped outside, the ground shook hard enough to
cause Slocum to stagger. He caught himself against the
edge of the bunkhouse in time to brace for another huge
explosion. Before the last of the thunder had died away,
Slocum was running for the mouth of the Silver Emperor
Mine. Huge clouds of dust billowed from deep within the
mine, followed quickly by the sound of rock *tearing*.
Slocum winced at the noise because he knew incredible
forces were destroying the mine. The explosion had taken
out the best of the shoring, and now the remainder of the
mine shaft shuddered and shifted and fell in on itself.

"What happened?" he shouted at the man standing
numbly to one side of the mouth. The guard turned and
opened his mouth. No words came out. Then he screamed
and clapped his hands to his ears.

Slocum had no time to fool with the man. The explosion
had both stunned and deafened the sentry, making him
worthless for anything Slocum might want to do. Coughing, Slocum forced his way to the mouth and saw that the
dust was beginning to settle out, giving a faint glimpse into
the hell of a major rock fall.

A new gust of dust forced Slocum back, rubbing his
eyes to clear them. He spat a mouthful of dirt and then
turned to the guard, who was looking around wildly now.
His shock was fading, and Slocum needed information.

Slocum grabbed the man by the shoulders and shook. A
small dust cloud rose and fell quickly from the guard's
clothing.

"Anyone in there? Did anyone get trapped?"

"I saw them," the man got out. "They was fired. They
was folks who worked here, and they blew up the mine."

Slocum turned angry now. The fired miners thought they
could get revenge on Wilson by destroying the mine. But
he had a cold lump deep in his gut that refused to unknot.

"Is anybody trapped in there?"

The guard nodded dully.

"How many? Who?"

"Half dozen. Saw Herk with 'em. Said they was tryin' to find a case of dynamite that was missin'."

Slocum didn't have to guess what had happened to the box of explosives. The fired miners had taken it and used several sticks—maybe all of the case—to blast the mine.

"Get to the bunkhouse and bring back whoever's there. I just got in with nine men. There's got to be more of Wilson's bullyboys. Get them all. We've got to dig like prairie dogs if we want to reach the men trapped in that mine."

"They're dead. They gotta be. Nobody could live through that hell."

Slocum took a half step backward, then unloaded a punch that rocked him all the way to the heels. The shock blasted up his arm and through his shoulder into his body. But the blow decked the guard. The man flopped around, arms flailing, then he sat down hard. His eyes were glazed and his jaw slack.

"What'd ya do that for?"

"Those are your friends in there."

"Ain't none of my friends. Most all of them quit. I should, too."

Slocum launched a kick at the man's head that barely missed. The guard crashed flat on his back, staring up in fear at a raging John Slocum.

"You want to kill me!"

"I want you to get every last man in camp and bring them here. We've got a whale of a lot of work ahead if we're going to rescue the men in there. And at least one of them's *my* friend." Slocum was friendly with Herkimer and that put him ahead of most men in Wilson's employ. But more important than friends or enemies, nobody deserved to die in the dark of a mine collapse. Nobody.

"I'll fetch 'em," the guard said, getting to shaky feet. "Ain't none of 'em alive in there. Can't imagine how that'd happen."

Slocum kicked the man in the seat of the pants to get him moving, then turned to study the destruction in the mine. His heart sank when he saw how completely the blast had sealed the shaft. If Herkimer and any others were in there, they were likely to be under tons of rock.

Slocum heaved a sigh of resignation, then set to work pulling debris from the mine. It was going to be a long night.

13

Slocum wiped his raw, bloody hands on his jeans and stepped back to study the progress being made on opening the mouth of the Silver Emperor Mine. They had toiled throughout the night, the nine drunks he had brought back from Panamint City working harder, longer and more skillfully than he had any right to hope. But as much work as they had put in, the rock fall still plugged the mouth. Completely.

"We can't keep on goin' like this much longer, Mr. Slocum," complained one of the men who worked directly for Wilson. All of the owner's private police force had been slackers, needing constant urging to get back to the chore at hand. Slocum had even promised to shoot one of the men if he tried to leave, as he had said he would do because the work was pointless and too hard.

Slocum didn't argue. He was slowly coming to agree, though he hated to admit it. They might be better served putting a tombstone over the mouth of the mine with the trapped miners' names on it. It was a better grave than most of those still living were likely to get, Slocum included.

"What if you were trapped in there? Would you want me to give up and walk away?" Slocum saw the hesitation on the man's face. Then came the question he dreaded most because he couldn't answer it.

"How do we know any of 'em's still alive?"

Slocum lifted his face to the dawn-lit sky and bellowed, "Take a fifteen minute break, men."

A collective sigh of relief passed through the miners. Only one or two looked skeptical about slowing their work. Slocum recognized both of them as older miners who had probably lost other friends in cave-ins—or maybe had been trapped themselves and rescued through the diligent work of those outside the coffin of stone.

"You, you," Slocum said, striding forward and pointing to the pair of miners who had looked most aggrieved at stopping work. He clambered over the piles of rock they had moved. How little it seemed for eight hours of digging?

He flopped on his belly at the top of the pile and pointed at a small crevice that had opened in the roof of the mine.

"Anybody hear voices from in there?" Slocum asked.

"Nope, nuthin'," said the smaller of the two. His larger, quieter friend simply shook his shaggy head. It was as Slocum had feared.

"Any sound at all? Banging on metal? Anything coming along the tracks?"

"I put my ear to the track first thing," said the small miner. "All I heard was rocks bangin' down, like stones still falling."

"That's good," Slocum said.

"Why's that?" asked the large miner, scratching himself. "That means the roof's givin' way."

"It has to fall through empty space. That means there might be air pockets in there where men can still be alive."

"You got something there, Slocum," said the small miner. "You been thinkin' real hard on this, ain't ya?"

"We have to know whether we keep digging or do something else," Slocum said. "That crevice that opened on the roof looks to run deeper. If I squeeze through and see how far I can get, we might get closer to anybody trapped inside."

"You're too big," the miner said. "Hell, your head wouldn't fit in that narrow little crack." He was already stripping off his equipment belt. "I kin get in and back 'fore you can turn around."

"You're my ace in the hole," Slocum said, grabbing the small miner by the shoulder. "If I'm not back in twenty minutes, come looking for me."

"Kin I argue you outta this?"

"No," Slocum said, grinning. "Get a rope. I want to tie it around my waist so you can pull me back." He hoped, if it were necessary to drag him out of the mine, that he would still be breathing as they plucked him from the rock tunnel. "Keep the rest of those galoots from sneaking off." Slocum jerked his thumb in the direction of the miners, now collapsed and struggling to regain their strength. When they did, they'd start talking, someone would suggest giving up, and the rest would eventually go along because it was easier to give up hope than it was to keep digging. Slocum wasn't likely to be back before that happened.

Slocum stared at the dark slash in the rock and shivered, in spite of the mounting temperature from the sun rising above the distant mountains. He cinched the rope tighter around his middle, then tossed aside his hat and gun belt before wiggling into the crevice. The going was tough, but Slocum kept at it, moving inch by inch until he got to a point where a chimney rose to the blue sky above and the fissure angled down into the heart of the mountain.

"Hello!" shouted Slocum. He waited for a moment, then called, "Anybody there?"

No words came in answer but he heard a distinct clicking noise, as if a hammer fell weakly against rock. The rhythm told Slocum that someone still lived, and this wasn't some cruel trick of nature.

"Coming down," Slocum called ahead. He headed straight down the fissure, knowing that his return had to be done by the miners pulling on the rope. There was not likely to be any hope of inching backward up the slope. He worked another twenty yards, quickly covered in sweat and grime. His hands were bleeding as he dragged himself along, sometimes pulling with little more than his fingertips. Slocum fought down panic as he went deeper into the mine, trying not to imagine himself being crushed to death in the dark. He had considered bringing a miner's candle, but the smoke from it would have choked him. Now he was glad he hadn't because it required both hands to scrape his way ever lower.

"Herkimer?" he called. "You there? Rap three times, if you are."

Slocum's heart almost leaped form his chest when he got three distinct, separate clicks. This lent speed to his advance.

He let out a cry of surprise when part of the crevice gave way under him. The rock tumbled downward a good five feet, leaving a hole the size of his head.

"Slocum? That you?" came a voice he recognized.

"The crevice gave way, just a little," Slocum answered Herkimer. "Can you see me?"

"Ain't got candles. Don't want to light 'em, even if we had 'em. Air'd go bad too fast."

Slocum began wiggling back and reached the spot where the rock had given way beneath him. He pressed his face downward through a hole hardly the size of a saucer. The air trapped in the chamber was stale but still breathable. Slocum realized he might be plugging up the only source of air for the men by coming down the crevice.

"How many of you?"

"Jist me and Nick and ole man Summers. He's shore in a bad way. Got all stove up when a rock fell on his chest. Don't think he's breathin' too good."

"Can you and Nick open this hole and crawl out?"

"Think I know where you're talkin' from," Herkimer said. "Get back and let us pickax at it a spell."

Slocum found himself in a fix. He couldn't go back any more than he had already. Try as he might he couldn't negotiate the upward slope without turning around. He tugged on the line, hoping the miners outside would respond by pulling him away from the hole. He jerked hard several times but got no response. Cursing, Slocum thought through his dilemma.

If he couldn't help opening the crevice to the chamber and he couldn't back up, he had only one course of action.

"I'm trapped, too," Slocum told Herkimer. "I'll crawl a ways farther and let you chisel at the hole. I'll have to back up and drop down to join you, so I can turn around to get out of here."

"All right. Let me know when you're clear," Herkimer said.

Slocum scooted forward and then called to the miners beneath him. The rock all around him began to quiver and ring with the force of the picks working. Slocum coughed as dust filled the narrow crevice, sifting downward to surround him. Worst of all, he couldn't get his hands back to wipe the grit from his eyes or clear his nose. He sneezed, and it was pure torture not to be able to scratch as the itch increased.

Then he let out a cry of surprise. The crevice suddenly opened, and he fell facedown. The chamber floor smashed Slocum a split second later, taking away his breath.

He felt hands fumbling to find his arms and pull him to a sitting position.

"You damn near fell on Summers," complained a voice that Slocum reckoned to be Nick since it wasn't Herkimer. "You still in one piece?"

"Let the man talk," Herkimer said.

Slocum looked around, but it was as dark as the inside of a buzzard's belly and didn't smell half as good. He got his breath back, hesitantly reached out and felt rock. He braced himself against it.

"I'm all right. You two up to wiggling through a tiny chimney to get out of here?"

"I was born that way," said Nick. "I don't think I'll have no trouble."

"Then get going. Follow the rope back, if you come to a junction. I didn't feel any on the way down, but I was homing in on Herkimer's voice below."

"Follow the rope," Nick said, his voice cracking with emotion. "Them's the finest words anybody ever said to me."

"Get going," Herkimer said. "Me and Slocum will be along in a few minutes."

"Better let him have ten, fifteen minutes head start," Slocum advised. "You don't want to get a face full of his boots or dirt from him kicking his way up."

"Bloody good thinkin', Slocum. But then you have a good head on your shoulders." Herkimer fell silent for a moment, then said, "What are we gonna do about Summers? He's in a bad way. Ain't been conscious since the cave-in, and there ain't no way he's gonna make it out on his own."

"It wasn't a cave-in," Slocum said. "Somebody dynamited the tunnel."

"Who'd do that?" Herkimer's voice was low and calm, but the tension Slocum felt told the real story. Given the chance to be alone with whoever lit the fuse, Herkimer would rip the miscreant limb from limb.

"Don't know but it might have been one of the men Wilson fired."

"That explains a bunch," Herkimer said. "We found sabotaged equipment all day long. That's why me and the other two came into the mine. Somebody'd tore up a section of track and an ore cart had derailed. We'd jist got the cart back onto the track and set to work on the track when the roof caved in." Herkimer paused a moment and changed his words. "When the damn dynamite went off."

"We'll find who did this," Slocum promised. "Not sure I'd go along with stringing them up, but that might be all we can do. There's not a lawman within a hundred miles."

"None worth his salt," Herkimer said. "There's a sheriff out of Panamint City, but he spends all his time serving process and collecting taxes. Ain't 'rested nobody I ever heard."

"You get on out of here and tell the men that I'll fasten the rope around Summers. They'll have to pull him out. I'll follow and make sure he doesn't get caught on any rock along the way."

"Mighty dangerous way to go, Slocum. You kin leave him and send somebody else in. Doc Lonigan could—"

"If Summers is in as bad shape as you say, he has to get out of the mine fast," Slocum said. "I'll tie the rope around his ankles so he gets pulled out feet first. That'll keep his head from banging along the way."

"Hope them boots of his don't fall off," Herkimer said with a chuckle.

"If nothing but the boots come out on the other side, you'll have a real dangerous chore ahead of you."

"What's that?" Herkimer asked.

"You'll have to go back into the crevice and breathe the air polluted by his smelly feet." Slocum got the response he wanted. Herkimer laughed boisterously.

"That's a good one, Slocum. Wait 'till I tell 'em out there."

"Get going," Slocum said, wondering how long it had been since Nick left. All sense of time vanished in the complete darkness.

Herkimer cursed as he stumbled over a pickax, then he got into the crevice.

"Hope I'm headin' in the right direction. My head's above my feet, so I must be goin' toward Heaven." With another laugh of joyous relief at being free of the chamber, the miner set off, making rustling noises in the crevice that sounded like rats scurrying. Slocum waited for what seemed an eternity, then dragged Summers over, untied the rope from around his own waist and secured it to the miner's ankles.

Grunting, Slocum got Summers up into the crevice, feet going upslope. He snapped the rope a couple times, then felt a jerk in reply to give him the go-ahead. Slocum put his shoulder against Summer's, shoved hard and the miner began slowly sliding out of the chamber after Herkimer. Slocum wasted no time following. He put his hands against the miner's shoulders and pushed, helping move him along the crevice for what seemed a century. When Slocum finally popped out of the narrow rock tunnel, the bright light hurt his eyes and the heat hit him like a hammer blow.

A huge cheer went up. Slocum was so dazed it took a few seconds to realize they were cheering him.

"Back, don't crowd, give the man some breathing room," came Lonigan's sharp voice. "He *wants* to be in the sun, don't you, Slocum?"

"Never thought I'd see it again," Slocum said honestly, squinting. "How's Summers doing?"

Doc Lonigan fell silent and looked away. Slocum peered up at him and knew the answer.

"He was mighty bad crushed," Herkimer said. "You done what you could."

"If I'd left him there and—"

"He was probably dead before you got him out," Lonigan said. "No good way of telling that, not if what Herkimer and Nick say's true about it being dark in there and all."

"It was darker 'n—"

"Never mind," Slocum said, his elation at being free of the mine vanishing like water on a hot rock. He had felt a surge of energy after freeing himself from the crevice but now only tiredness filled him like some evil brew.

"You saved two men. That's more 'n any of the rest of us woulda accomplished," said the small miner who had volunteered to go in place of Slocum. "You're a damned hero, Slocum. Act like one!"

A cheer went up again as Lonigan and Herkimer helped Slocum to his feet. He grabbed his hat and pulled it down around his eyes, the brim shielding his eyes from the intense light. Another miner passed him his holster so he could strap it on. He felt better, but the loss of Summers rankled.

"Slocum, thank God you're all right. You saved my men. Thank you."

Slocum squinted and turned to see Big Pete Wilson

coming up the slope strewn with rock from the attempt to open the mine.

"Where were you?" Slocum asked bluntly.

"I was at the smelter. There were . . . problems."

"Sabotage?"

"Yes," Wilson said bitterly. "Some of the fired miners are responsible. I know it. Did they do this, too?"

"That's what Slocum there thinks," Herkimer piped up. "If I get my hands on any of 'em, they're headed for the Promised Land!"

"Not that direction, not if I find 'em first," Nick said, as angry as Herkimer.

"There's no easy way of finding who did it," Slocum said. "They made quite a mess."

"Been lookin' it over," Herkimer cut in. "Going back down the tunnel where we went before's not a good idea, but if we cut in from an angle, we kin follow the new vein of ore and work back to the older one. It was close to petered out, but the new one! That's a rich vein of carbonate."

"You sound like a man who knows his job. You're the new mine super," Wilson said. "And you're still my foreman, Slocum. I owe you for this. I do."

A thousand questions crowded into Slocum's brain, but he was too exhausted to get them all lined up and marched out for Wilson to answer.

"Things'll change around here, yes, sir," Wilson said grimly. "This isn't going to happen again."

"How're they going to change?" Slocum asked, but Wilson was already a delivering a speech to his men, praising them, praising Slocum, promising better conditions.

Slocum sat on a rock and wondered what the hell was going on.

14

Slocum sat in the shade of the tall building, sipping water from a jug and wishing he were anywhere else. Wilson had put him in charge of guarding the smelter. It made sense, in a way, but Slocum didn't like it. The smelter turned out the first valuable silver bars, and anything happening here robbed the mine owner of all his hard-won metal. But it was boring. From all he could tell, there hadn't been any sabotage at the smelter when Wilson had ridden over a couple days earlier. The real damage had been done at the Silver Emperor.

Some equipment had failed, and that was it. It needed maintenance it hadn't received and simply broke through hard usage. So now Slocum was guarding the smelter, its equipment and the slow but steady outpouring of silver refined from the mountain of ore nearby.

It would be quite a while before new ore piled atop the old, but not as long as it might have been without Herkimer, Nick and the others. The sabotage—and the death of Summers—had galvanized the miners into putting in twice the amount of work they might have, otherwise. Slocum shook his head. If he hadn't doubted Wilson was capable of it, he would have thought the whole thing was a plot to get more work from the miners. But what was Wilson capable of doing? To that Slocum had no answer.

Instead, he sat in the dubious shade, drank water and watched as the smelter workers moved one bar of silver after another from the heated interior of the shed to a tank where they plunged the hot metal before stacking it in a case for transportation.

Slocum found himself nodding off, only to jerk awake when he heard the rumble of wagon wheels along the rocky road leading to the smelter. He heaved himself to his feet and brushed off the dirt the best he could. He hadn't expected a shipment to be made so soon because there were only two crates of silver bars—about $3000 worth. When Slocum saw the driver and the guards, he felt his bile rising. They were the bullyboys Wilson had used to chase off the regular miners.

"You got the boxes ready for us, Slocum?" called the big stupid one who was the trio's leader.

"Only two," Slocum answered. He hitched up his gun belt as he strode forward. "Why're you so eager to move out such a small amount, Jerrold?"

"The boss says we got to get it to the banker in town right away."

Slocum remembered the bank president's curious way of passing along the information to Wilson that the silver was needed in San Francisco. It had been more than a simple request. It had been an outright demand.

"Be two, three more days to get another crate of bars smelted," Slocum said. "Why not wait for that?"

"We're going now," Jerrold said. He sneered. "You don't like it, take it up with the boss."

"Let me get my horse," Slocum said. Jerrold's eyes narrowed as he studied Slocum.

"Where you goin'?"

"If you take the two crates of silver bars, there's no reason for me to stay here with nothing to guard. So I'll ride along to Panamint City just to be sure nothing happens to the silver." Slocum saw this didn't sit well with Jerrold, but there wasn't much he could say about it. Slocum's job was known to one and all in the mining camp. He was responsible for guarding the precious metal pulled from the earth. While it didn't amount to a hill of beans, he was also mine foreman. That required him to do something more than sit on his butt in the hot sun and watch men working to reduce the silver ore into shiny bars.

"You don't hafta go," Jerrold said.

"I know, but I want to. Any complaints?" Slocum's cold green eyes fixed on Jerrold's watery blue ones. Jerrold shook his head a little too fast, a little too hard. He did object but could say nothing about it.

"Get the crates loaded. There they are," Slocum said, pointing out the pair of silver-laden boxes. He saddled his horse, let it drink a spell, then swung into the saddle. Jerrold and his cronies were already rattling along the road toward Panamint City, but it took Slocum only a few minutes to catch up and get out of the dust cloud behind the wagon. Jerrold rode to the left while Slocum rode to the right. The other two, driver and shotgun guard, sat uneasily in the driver's box, necks craning around as if looking for trouble.

They probably were expecting the worst. Slocum hadn't heard that any of the patrols Wilson had sent out to capture the Mojave Guns had been successful. If the men in those posses weren't any smarter than Jerrold, the road agents had nothing to fear.

"You expectin' trouble, Slocum?" called the guard. He wiped his mouth with the back of his sleeve and looked badly in need of a shot or two of whiskey. His hands shook a mite, and his bloodshot eyes rolled around in his head like fancy marbles.

"Until the outlaws are caught, they'll work this road and try to hijack every shipment they can." Slocum knew silver bars rode in these two crates. He wondered if Jerrold's orders had been to return to the camp with the silver where it could be switched for crates with worthless rock for the road agents to "steal" again.

The guard twisted half around on the bench seat and looked behind, as if he could see through the dust cloud. The way the driver acted put Slocum on edge. Something was wrong, and they weren't sharing their suspicions—or what they knew for certain. Slocum reached down and made sure his Winchester was easily slipped from its scabbard.

The driver slowed as they came to the rocky cut in the road where the Mojave Guns had tried to ambush the shipment before. Slocum motioned for Jerrold to ride out wide, and he would do the same on the right side. That way they could scout around the rocks and flush out anyone foolish enough to lay a trap here for a second time.

Slocum came around the rocks and urged his horse up a steep, gravelly slope back to the road when he heard gunfire. He sawed at the reins and got his horse headed back down the road in the direction of the wagon.

He galloped to the wagon in time to see the guard drop his shotgun, slump and then fall over the side to the ground. A second flurry of bullets tore through the side of the wagon. The driver yelped like a stuck pig and grabbed for his thigh. He dropped the reins and the mules brayed noisily, then tried to go their separate ways. Slocum was thankful that Wilson didn't use horses on this route. They would have bolted and stopping the runaway team would have been a matter of finding pieces of the broken wagon later.

With a smooth movement, Slocum got his rifle from its scabbard, raised the stock to his shoulder and fired. The recoil hurt his shoulder, reminding him of the abrasions and scratches he had accumulated sliding into the mine to rescue Herkimer and Nick. He was pleased when he saw an outlaw slump back behind a rock. The road agent might have been dead or just winged—it didn't matter to Slocum since the man was out of the fight.

To his surprise, three other road agents closed in from the far side of the wagon. He wondered what had happened to Jerrold, then he was fighting for his life. The stupid guard might have fallen prey to the road agents, or he might have thrown in with them, for all Slocum knew.

He fired methodically and kept the three highwaymen

occupied, but his magazine came up empty, forcing him to draw his six-shooter and blaze away with that.

"You able to drive?" he called. The driver, now pale and shaky, shook his head. Slocum saw the steady drip of the man's blood from the bottom of the box and knew the round he had taken must have cut an artery in his leg. The driver was dying fast as he filled up the driver's box with his life's blood.

Slocum rode closer and brought his six-gun to bear on . . . Rafe Van Winkle. He hesitated a split second, then squeezed the trigger. Perfect sight picture. Front blade on the center of Rafe's chest. No way to miss at this range. But the hammer fell on a spent chamber.

A commotion back along the road distracted both Slocum and Rafe for an instant. Jerrold rode hellbent for leather, followed by three men wildly firing. Slocum looked back and his eyes locked with Rafe's. Each thought exactly what the other was thinking. Slocum thought the men behind Jerrold were coming to Rafe's aid, and Rafe thought they were coming after him.

Rafe Van Winkle was right.

"Git 'em, boys. Shoot 'em up good!" shouted Jerrold. He waved his six-shooter around wildly, spraying lead in unpredictable directions. Slocum wasn't sure if that had scared off Rafe and the others or if they had decided to abandon their robbery for other reasons. He watched in silent rage as Rafe and three other outlaws hightailed it. He shoved his six-shooter back into his holster and turned his horse to face Jerrold and the trio behind him.

"Who the hell are they and where did you go?" demanded Slocum.

"They work for Big Pete," Jerrold said. "They do what I tell 'em, and I went to alert 'em to the robbery."

"If you'd stayed with the silver shipment your two other friends might still be alive." Slocum angrily pointed to where the shotgun guard lay dead and then to the driver, slumped in a pool of his own blood in the driver's box.

"I had to fetch 'em. They was trailin' us, waitin' for them sonsabitches to try robbin' the shipment."

"Get the shipment on into Panamint City," Slocum said.

"No!"

Slocum rode over and glared at Jerrold until the man wilted. "You got it all wrong," Slocum said coldly. "I'm foreman. These three will drive the wagon, with the silver, into town and make sure it gets into the bank. And they'll get a written receipt for the silver from the bank president. Now!"

The three looked at Jerrold, as if he gave the orders.

"Get the damned wagon into town!" raged Slocum. This time the trio jumped to it, only to slow and argue about who was to drive. Slocum grabbed the nearest man by the collar and lifted. He half-threw the man into the driver's box and said, "You drive. Now!"

They still hesitated until Slocum drew his ebony-handled six-gun and laid it across the saddle in front of him. This decided them. The man he had chosen as driver got the mules pulling and the other two rode guard, one on each side of the wagon. As they rumbled through the notch between the boulders Slocum was coming to think of as Ambush Rocks, he considered calling for them to stop so he could check the crates to be certain they still carried silver bars. He held his tongue, though, as he thought on it. Rafe and his gang weren't stupid. If Jerrold had switched crates at the smelter, Rafe would have known and stolen the silver stashed there. That he had come out on the road to ambush the shipment said it was legitimate.

Unlike the other, which had been hidden behind Wilson's shack.

"What are you waiting for?" Slocum demanded of Jerrold. "Get after the shipment. Protect it."

"Nope, I'm goin' after the road agents," Jerrold said. "Big Pete tole me to bring him back a couple scalps, no matter what."

"No matter that you'll get a bullet in your damn gut because you didn't obey my orders?" Slocum lifted the Colt Navy and aimed it in Jerrold's direction.

"I take orders from the boss, not you." Jerrold hesitated, judging how likely Slocum was to shoot him out of the saddle. Something decided Jerrold. "I'm goin' after 'em now. You with me or agin me?"

"There are three of them against the pair of us," Slocum said.

"You can pick which one you want. I'm more 'n a match for any two of them snakes."

Slocum knew Jerrold overestimated his own abilities, but he said nothing. He gestured with his pistol for the man to ride on after the outlaws. Jerrold let out a whoop of glee and galloped off. Slocum followed at a more leisurely pace, taking the time to reload both his six-gun and his rifle. He watched the trail carefully, trying to see past the way Jerrold had obscured the outlaws' hoofprints with his own headlong pursuit. Slocum turned wary when he saw how two of the outlaws had split from the third.

"Jerrold!" he called. "You're on the wrong trail." Slocum recognized the hoofprints left by the solitary road agent Jerrold followed. Slocum wasn't sure why he wanted to protect Rafe Van Winkle, but if he could avoid telling Mira that Rafe had died, Slocum would do what he could.

"What? Whatya sayin', Slocum?" Jerrold rode back, his horse staggered from exhaustion, its flanks lathered.

"Look at the spoor. They went that way." Slocum pointed out the two sets of hoofprints leading up into the hills.

"You're right. You got a keen eye fer this."

Slocum shrugged off the compliment.

"My horse has started to limp. If we can wait a spell, I can find out if its going lame or just picked up a stone in its shoe." Slocum waited to see how the lie would sit with Jerrold. It worked better than he had any right to expect.

"We can't let 'em get too far ahead, Slocum. They'll get away."

"My horse . . ."

"Screw your horse," Jerrold said. "Big Pete gave me orders to get one or two of them varmints, and I am!" With that Jerrold cruelly spurred his horse on the uphill trail after the pair of outlaws. Slocum had no love for the members of the Mojave Guns gang, but he had even less for Jerrold. Maybe all three would shoot it out, and all of them would end up buzzard bait.

He dismounted to rest his horse, waited a spell, then mounted and rode after Rafe Van Winkle. Slocum knew he was riding into a trap five minutes before he saw how poorly Rafe had planned it. Before the outlaw could shoot him from the saddle, Slocum bent low, slid to the far side of his horse and trotted ahead.

When he got even with where Rafe was going crazy trying to get a clear shot at his quarry, Slocum dropped off. He hit the ground, stumbled and then had his Colt out, cocked and aimed. Rafe's muzzle was out of line. All Slocum had to do was squeeze off a shot; Rafe had to turn, aim and fire.

"Drop it or I'll drop you," Slocum said. "It's damn hot out here in the sun, and I've seen 'bout all the killing for one day that I care to."

"They wasn't supposed to die like that. But they shot back instead of givin' up," Rafe said, almost whining.

"Drop your smoke wagon," Slocum said. Rafe obeyed. "Now get those hands way up high so I can see them."

Slocum walked over, made sure Rafe didn't have a hideout gun secreted on him, then whistled, got his horse to trot back and used his lariat to tie up the outlaw.

"What now? String me up from the nearest tree?" Rafe sounded bitter, and Slocum reckoned he had good reason.

"I'm going to do worse than stretch your neck," Slocum said.

"Drag me behind your horse for a few miles? Stake me out in the sun to die after cutting off my eyelids?"

"Worse than any Apache torture," Slocum assured him. He tugged on the rope, pulled Rafe along and found his horse. He let the outlaw mount and then rode ahead just fast enough to keep the rope taut to prevent any escape.

"What're you gonna do to me?"

"I'm taking you to your sister," Slocum said. "Might be, I'll take you to your pa."

"No!"

Slocum almost laughed at the reaction. Rafe Van Winkle preferred to be staked out under the Death Valley sun to being turned over to his blood kin. Rafe fell into a sullen silence as they reached the road going down the middle of Wildrose Canyon, then took the branch going out to the kilns.

"Don't do this. You don't understand."

"You're right," Slocum said. "Why not tell me what's gone wrong between you and your relatives?"

"They wouldn't understand," Rafe said.

"I'm smart enough to have caught you. Tell me."

"My ma—" started Rafe, then he clamped his mouth shut when Mira Van Winkle came out of a shack and spotted them.

"Rafe!" she cried. The woman's bright eyes widened when she saw the rope pinning her brother's arms to his side curving over to where the other end was wrapped around Slocum's saddle horn.

"Brought you a present, Mira," Slocum said. "What do you want to do with him?"

"What've you been up to, Rafe?"

When no answer was forthcoming, Slocum told her of the ambush and attempted robbery.

"If Wilson or his bullyboys catch you, they'll hang you for sure," Mira said. She looked at Slocum. "Or are you going to do that for Wilson?"

"I've got some questions of Mr. Wilson that are begging for answers," Slocum said. "I don't feel too good about turning over anybody trying to rob his silver shipments until I get some answers."

"You're letting me go?" asked Rafe.

"Didn't say that." Slocum unwrapped the rope from around the horn and tossed the end to Mira, who deftly caught it. She braced her feet, reared back and jerked for all she was worth. Slocum knew she was a strong woman, and she proved it by the ease with which she pulled her brother from the saddle. Rafe Van Winkle hit the ground hard enough to stun him.

"You go on into my place, John. I want to talk with my brother." Mira kicked Rafe in the ribs and rolled him over. He sputtered and struggled, but she kept the rope tight enough to prevent him from recovering his balance.

Slocum walked to the small cabin, dismounted and watered his horse before hobbling it over to the shade of the cabin. Only then did he go inside. He had to smile as he watched Mira giving Rafe a tongue-lashing. Then he sobered, wondering what he ought to do. He had no idea why he didn't turn Rafe over to Wilson. The Mojave Guns had robbed and killed along the road to Panamint City ever since he had drifted into Death Valley, and Slocum had taken his share of bullets at their hands. But Rafe seemed to be driven by something more than simple greed. He wanted revenge on Wilson for something he wouldn't say.

The scars were only a part of it, and if Slocum was any judge, they were an insignificant part.

Rafe looked like a small child being scolded by his mother. Whatever Mira said to him reduced him more and more until Slocum saw the explosion coming. No man took that kind of criticism forever.

"Mira!" he called, waving her over. The dark-haired woman glanced in his direction, back at her brother, then came over.

"What is it, John? I'm not finished with him. I'm not even started!"

"Yes, you are. If you haven't made your point by now, you never will. Why's Rafe so intent on getting revenge on Wilson? What's Wilson done to deserve it? Must be powerful bad for it to fester for years."

"He won't tell me." Mira looked back where Rafe stood, shoulders slumped, but Slocum saw the spine coming back to the outlaw.

"Until you find out, he's not going to stop. Maybe he won't stop even then."

"I ought to tell Pa."

"Rafe and your pa haven't spoken in years, have they? I'm not sure if Sebastian doesn't think his son's dead."

Emotions played over Mira's face. She took a deep breath, then let it out.

"What are you going to do with him? With Rafe?"

"Don't know if I've seen him lately. I tried chasing down an outlaw, but he got away." Slocum's green eyes locked with Mira's clear blue ones.

"Oh," she said. "Don't go running off." Mira hurried back to Rafe and spoke sternly to him a few more seconds, then pointed in Slocum's direction. Rafe hesitated, then grabbed his horse's reins, mounted and rode off in a powerful hurry. Slocum didn't blame him much. Jerrold was still on his trail, the man who had caught him stood a few yards off—and his sister had chewed him out.

Slocum watched Mira sashay back, appreciating the little twitches she put into her behind, just for his appreciation. She sucked in a deep breath again, making sure her breasts rose and fell just right. For Slocum, any movement there would be fine. But Mira made sure it was better than fine—and just for him.

She stopped in front of him, her face turned up slightly and her petal-shaped lips parted the smallest amount.

"Is it all right that I let Rafe ride out?"

"Is this all right?" Slocum countered. He put his hands around her waist and drew her closer, then kissed her. There was no resistance at all. Mira returned the kiss with ardor.

"More than all right," she said, gasping when she broke off the kiss. "Is this why you brought Rafe to me. So you and I could . . . ?"

"Could what?" Slocum bent down again and nibbled at her earlobe and then whispered, "Do this? Or maybe this?" He tongued his way down from her ear past her slender throat to the neckline of her blouse. He unbuttoned the top button and kissed and licked the flesh revealed. Then he undid another button and licked and kissed lower.

By the time her blouse hung open, her firm young breasts were exposed to the midday Death Valley heat. But the real heat came from the oral attention he gave to those scrumptious mounds of flesh. First he kissed the nipple capping one and then hurried to give the other equal attention. When he tried sucking in the entire mountain of white flesh, Mira arched her back and tried to jam even more into his mouth.

Slocum took full advantage of this. He tongued her rockhard nipple, then backed off so he could suckle on it. The rubbery hardness increased as excited blood pumped into the nub. He rolled it around with his tongue, then nipped lightly with his teeth. He felt Mira go weak in the knees. His arms around her waist supported her as he meted out similar erotic punishment to her other breast.

"Oh, John, I—" She never got any farther. Her knees sagged again. This time he reached down and caught her up, kicked open the cabin door and went inside.

It was twenty degrees cooler out of the sun, but Slocum intended for it to heat up mighty fast. He spun Mira around so her hair flew out in a thick, dark banner and then dropped her on the bed. She hit, swung around and lifted her knees, placing her feet flat on the bed. Looking boldly at him between her knees, she began pulling back her skirt a little bit at a time.

Her shoes came into view. Then her trim ankles. Her calves were more than Slocum could resist. He dropped down and kissed them. For a moment, the lovely woman hesitated in her slow revelations, then continued. Slocum worked his way up as more of her slender legs was revealed to his lusting gaze. He kissed the insides of her thighs until her legs opened to him involuntarily.

"Oh, John," she sobbed when he worked even higher up her legs, to the delightful nest hidden between her legs. She dropped flat on the bed, gasping for breath when he thrust his tongue deep within her molten center. He controlled her

with just the tip of his tongue, lifting her hips off the bed and
then letting her fall back heavily when he slipped wetly free.

"Mighty fine artesian spring I've found. Mighty tasty."

"Help yourself. Don't . . . oh, yes, yes!"

Slocum wasn't waiting for her to give a long speech.
She had told him how much she liked his oral attentions—
and he liked giving them to her. He lapped long and slow
from one end of her nether lips to the other, then caught the
tiny bud of pink flesh popping up at the juncture. Sucking
it into his mouth drove the woman wild. Or so he thought.
She really went berserk when he flicked the tip of his
tongue back and forth as fast as he could.

One instant Mira was shrieking with need. The next
Slocum heard nothing. The woman's thighs clamped firmly
over his ears, pinning his head firmly in place. He did what
he could to breath, but mostly he sent his tongue sailing in
and out, sampling the heady wine seeping from within.
Then his own needs grew and made him uncomfortable.

As the legs relaxed, he pulled back, got to his feet and
towered above her. Never had Slocum seen a prettier sight.
Mira's hair was in wild disarray, fanned out over the bed.
Her knees were still drawn up revealing her most intimate
places to him as her skirt bunched around her waist. He
dropped his gun belt and unfastened his jeans.

Her eyes widened as she saw the length and girth jutting
from his waist.

He dropped to the bed between her legs and moved forward. She eagerly grasped his thick stalk and drew it down,
down to the pink, scalloped gates to her interior. He toyed
with her for a moment, drawing himself up and down the
length where his mouth had been only seconds earlier, then
he was no longer able to restrain himself.

He moved forward a little more, feeling himself slip between her fingers and into the clutching heat of her most
intimate niche. Surrounded, he reveled in the heat and
moisture as long as he could. Then he levered his hips forward and sank all the way inward. The impact of their bod-

ies colliding sent a shock wave through his loins. For the woman, it was even more intense.

She gaped, clutched at him, then fell back, arched her back and ground her crotch into his. She stirred his fleshy wand about within her, then sank back, face gleaming with sweat.

"Do it, John. Do it. Oh, please, don't stop now."

"Do this?" he teased. He rotated his hips and felt himself stroking over her tender, clinging insides. Then he withdrew inch by inch, tormenting her as he went with the promise of more to come. When only the thick head of his manhood remained within her, he paused, got his breath back and then plunged forward.

Slow, powerful strokes built their desires to the breaking point—but Slocum wanted more. He kept up the pace until he was on the verge of losing control, then changed the tempo to short, quick strokes. The friction of his flesh against hers ignited passions that were slumbering in the woman's trim body.

Mira shrieked in pleasure and thrashed about, impaled on his fleshy spike. As she returned from the delightful lands where Slocum had just sent her, he picked up the pace even more. The heat mounted within and set fire to their bodies, their emotions and minds. He struggled to hold back the white-hot tide building deep within his loins, but he was only flesh and blood. Everything added to the thrill of this encounter: Mira panting heavily and getting all lathered up below him; her fingers clutched and clawed at his upper arms, supporting him on the bed as he looked down into her lust-glazed bright blue eyes. But the heat down low as he stroked pushed him over the edge.

He heard Mira calling out again as if from afar but the roar in his ears drowned out any real sounds. He arched his back and crammed himself forward with as much force and speed as he could. She took him willingly and then locked her legs around his waist to keep him from getting away. Melded into one, they rolled on the bed, their passions surging and soaring, flying and eventually floating gently back to earth.

Sweaty, tired, and sated Slocum looked into the woman's face.

She smiled almost shyly, then the look changed to the wicked one he usually saw when they were together.

"Ready?" she asked.

"No! Not so soon. I'm not made out of steel!"

"You could have fooled me. No, wait, you're right. Steel's never so pleasurable." She gripped him firmly, but he had turned flaccid. No matter there were small, distinct stirrings, he was spent. For the moment.

They lay side by side on the small bed, exploring one another's body with deliberation as the sun set and the temperature dropped rapidly, until Mira's fingers began to produce more than a faint stirring. She showed him what it meant to anneal a steel spike in a fleshy blast furnace.

By the time Slocum left Mira's cabin after midnight, he was mighty glad he had brought Rafe Van Winkle here. Even if it meant a passel of trouble later on.

15

Dawn lit the eastern sky behind the mountains as Slocum rode back to the Silver Emperor Mine. He drew rein and stared when he saw Jerrold and the three men who had gone on with the silver shipment lounging in the wagon parked beside the road. Jerrold whittled away at a piece of pine while the other two dozed. Slocum couldn't take his eyes off the flashing blade as it caught the first rays of day. One after another of the curlicues flew off the stick as Jerrold whittled faster, taking out his anger on the inanimate wood.

Slocum had the feeling Jerrold and the other two were waiting for something—and his gut told him who that might be. He slipped the leather thong off the hammer of his Colt, made sure the six-shooter slid easily and only then did he ride slowly toward the trio.

Both of Jerrold's partners sat up and rubbed sleep from their eyes at the sound of his horse's hooves.

"Morning," Slocum greeted, intending to ride past.

"Where'd you go, Slocum?" demanded Jerrold. "Where you been since yesterday afternoon?"

"Looking for outlaws. It doesn't look to me that you had any more luck than I did finding any."

Jerrold swung the thick-bladed knife around and pointed with it. Slocum saw only the merest sliver of steel because the tip was aimed straight at his eyes.

137

"Gents, this here's the man who's in cahoots with them Mojave Guns," Jerrold said loudly. "Now what are we gonna do 'bout that?"

"String 'im up," suggested the smaller of the two men.

"Shoot him where he sits," said the other, larger one, reaching for his six-shooter. He was big and he was slow. He was also dead.

Slocum cleared leather and got off an accurate shot that hit the man square in the center of the chest. The man shifted his weight in the wagon bed, looked down at the red spot slowly growing on his shirt and then keeled over without uttering another word.

"Don't try it," Slocum said, swinging his pistol around to cover Jerrold. "That was a damn fool thing to do. In fact, it was so stupid I think you put him up to it."

"You're in cahoots with them!" repeated Jerrold.

"Why? Because you couldn't find the two you went after?"

"You found one and you let 'im go!"

"What makes you think that?" Slocum remained cool but wondered if Jerrold or his partners had been spying on him and Mira. If so, they knew more than he cared for them to know.

"Put that hogleg away. You ain't gonna kill nobody else," Jerrold said.

Slocum foolishly started to obey. The other gunman flopped onto his back and pulled his six-shooter while supine. He fired. The bullet tore another hole in the brim of Slocum's battered hat. But Slocum's return fire went wild because the mules hitched to the wagon had finally bestirred themselves enough to jerk hard at their harnesses. Slocum's round would have found its target if the wagon hadn't lurched. His bullet tore a hunk of wood from the side and then all hell broke loose.

Jerrold threw his knife with such accuracy that Slocum's left arm went numb as a gash opened high on his biceps. He turned, doubled over, then brought his six-gun around again. He fired twice more, exchanging rounds with Jerrold's partner. He missed both times—and Jerrold was dragging his six-shooter from its holster.

Slocum ducked low, used his knees to guide his horse back along the trail he had just ridden, then swerved sharply off the rutted road to avoid a hail of bullets from Jerrold and his partner. As he rode bent over, Slocum shoved his six-shooter back into its holster and struggled to pull his rifle from its scabbard. The bleeding cut on his left arm was turning painful, but worse than this was the way his blood made everything slick.

He could hardly hang onto his rifle as he swung it around and brought it to his shoulder. His left arm trembled with weakness and pain from the gash, but he got off a single round that settled one man's hash. The gunman in the wagon bed had climbed to his feet and was trying to get a bead on Slocum. He outlined himself against the rising sun and made a perfect target.

A perfect corpse.

Slocum awkwardly levered another round into the chamber to take out Jerrold, but he hesitated when he caught the glint of sunlight off metal back down the road. Slocum looked over his shoulder and saw a half dozen riders in the distance. A dozen possibilities flashed through Slocum's mind, but the only one that made sense was Wilson hiring an entire posse of gunslingers. They might have been recruited when Jerrold's partners went to Panamint City or they could have been hired in other ways. Whatever the explanation, Slocum had to act fast or he'd be caught in a crossfire.

Balancing his rifle the best he could, he got off another shot at Jerrold. He heard the man grunt, more in surprise than in pain. This encouraged Slocum to chamber another round and charge. He put his heels to his horse and made a full frontal assault that spooked Jerrold more than anything else might have. Jerrold tried to make a stand, but Slocum fired at point-blank range. The gunman grunted in pain this time.

Slocum rode past, wheeled about and almost fell from

his horse. The flowing wound was making him giddy. For a moment he thought he was going blind, then he realized Jerrold had hightailed it.

Slocum stood in the stirrups and peered back down the road. The riders he had seen before were gone—or perhaps they had rounded a bend in the road and were hidden for a few minutes. He hoped Jerrold hadn't seen them. If Jerrold and the other gunslingers teamed up, he would be dead in the blink of an eye. Thoughts spun in crazy circles in his head. He had to track Jerrold and stop him, as he had stopped the two jackals with him.

But Slocum wobbled too much to stay in the saddle for long. His arm burned like he had shoved it into one of Mira's charcoal kilns, and the heat was spreading into his chest. Light-headed, he turned his horse toward the camp and rode in.

"Hey, Slocum, what's wrong?"

"Got hurt," Slocum said. "Outlaws." That wasn't exactly right, but Slocum wasn't in any condition to bandy words. This would get the miner moving in the right direction.

"Hey, hey, Doc!" the miner shouted. "Got a wounded man out here. Doc Lonigan!"

The miner helped Slocum from the saddle. Slocum tried to stand, but his legs were too weak. He sagged onto the miner, who helped him into the shade of the nearby privy. Slocum sucked in a deep breath and tried to focus.

"Damnation, Slocum, if you get yourself any more banged up, I won't be able to patch you up."

"Hi, Doc," Slocum said. "Miss me?"

"Like a toothache," Lonigan said, ripping away Slocum's shirtsleeve. Slocum winced as the cloth also tore away part of the dried blood over the wound. Lonigan muttered and mumbled, then said, "This here's a knife cut. Or from something long and sharp. I expected you to be carryin' an extra ounce or two of lead instead of gettin' into a knife fight."

"Lot of ways to die out here," Slocum said.

"Well, today's not your day to cash in your chips." Lonigan jerked the bandage tighter on his arm and surveyed his handiwork. "You ought to get something to eat. Something that'll stick to your ribs. Tell Cookie to fix you a steak. We got some real meat around somewhere, if it's not gone bad yet from the heat."

"What's been going on in camp?" Slocum asked. "I'm gone a day and things . . . changed."

Lonigan snorted in disgust. "Wilson decided he needed his own private army. Heard-tell he's got the call out for every hard case and bounty hunter within a hundred miles. Wants to stop the Mojave Guns, he says, but he's not offering enough reward."

"That means anybody coming in just likes to kill," Slocum said, closing his eyes and leaning back. He saw the riders back on the road as clearly as if they were in front of him.

"Men like that," Lonigan said, seeing Slocum's interest. "I thought Jerrold was bad enough, him and his cronies. These men aren't likely to stop and figure out if they're killin' a miner or a road agent."

At the mention of Jerrold, Slocum stiffened. He had been drifting, the loss of blood and the stifling heat working to numb his mind. He had to catch Jerrold to keep him from telling Wilson about Rafe Van Winkle. If the mine owner thought for an instant that Slocum was aiding one of the gang, he would jump to the conclusion that Slocum was also a member of the Mojave Guns.

"Whoa, wait a second, Slocum. Where are you going?" Lonigan pushed him back down.

"Got to get on the trail and—"

"I told you to get some food. Then you ought to rest for a day or two to get your strength back." Lonigan studied him carefully. "What aren't you tellin' me, Slocum? What have *you* been up to in the last day or so?"

"Slocum! Glad to see you finally came back."

"Damnation," Lonigan muttered under his breath. "Just what we all need."

"Been out chasing down outlaws," Slocum said. He

waited for Big Pete Wilson to repeat the accusations Jerrold had made out on the road, but they weren't forthcoming.

"I got men hired to do that. I need you to drive the wagon over to the kilns and get more charcoal. Where's the damned wagon, anyway?"

"Down the road a ways," Slocum said. "I . . . saw it on my way back."

Wilson glared at him, noticing the torn sleeve and the drying blood on Slocum's shirt.

"You hurt bad?"

"Yeah," Lonigan said.

"No," Slocum said, louder. "I'm up for some driving."

"Then get your ass over to the kilns. The smelter's running low and we've got a couple tons of fresh mined ore to reduce."

"Right away," Slocum said.

"Mr. Wilson, Slocum's hurt bad," Lonigan said. "He needs to rest."

"I'm not paying him to loaf around. I'm not payin' you to do that, either, Lonigan. Get back to your job gradin' the ore."

"It's all right, Doc," Slocum said, using the privy wall as support so he could stand without keeling over. "I'll grab some food and be on my way."

Slocum spoke to Wilson's back. The man stalked off, shouting angrily at three miners he thought were malingering. Slocum ducked around the outhouse when the hired gunmen rode into camp, heads swivelling as they looked for him. Slocum knew they would figure out he had killed the two men back at the wagon the instant they spotted him. How could he explain a fresh knife wound otherwise? They wouldn't buy his story that he had tangled with the outlaws. They'd know.

If Jerrold rode back into camp, they'd know for certain.

Slocum went to the mess hall and got some food, ate a bit and stuffed more into a burlap bag before returning to his horse. Lonigan had gone back to his regular job. Slocum looked around for Herkimer or any of the other miners who might give him information about the mine and its recent operation. The best he could tell, a new shaft was being driven into the side of the mountain, about where he had suggested after being in the crevice to rescue Herkimer and Nick.

He mounted, considering what Wilson had told him about fetching more charcoal. Taking the Silver Emperor wagon was out of the question. To go back to it with the dead bodies would bring too much attention his way, especially now that the gunmen had come into camp. They might have left a guard on the wagon with its cargo of corpses while the rest reported to Wilson.

Slocum felt more than the heat of the Death Valley sun on him as he rode off. He cut across country, thinking to head off Jerrold as he considered how important it was to end the miserable snake's life. So what if he reported back to Wilson? Then another thought hit him. Slocum could be in Panamint City by sundown and in San Francisco in a couple days, leaving all the turmoil behind him.

But there were Mira Nell and her brother and the questions Rafe posed. Slocum doubted the answer to why Rafe hated Big Pete Wilson so much was worth getting ventilated over, but he hated to run out on Mira without saying good-bye. He owed her that much.

He turned toward the charcoal kilns, intending to approach from off-road but the longer he was in the saddle, the weaker he became. The heat used him as an anvil, pounding at his head and back as he slumped forward and he began wondering if the horse was going in circles, maybe even taking him back to the Silver Emperor Mine. If he ended up there, he wouldn't last a minute. Wilson's hired guns would cut him down.

"There, over there," he said weakly, guiding his horse toward a rock wall at the side of Wildrose Canyon. A few scraggly shrubs grew, hinting at the possibility of a small spring. More than water, though, Slocum wanted a place to stretch out and rest until the worst heat of the day had passed. Slocum almost fell from horseback, remembered to put hobbles on the horse and then sat heavily, back against the hot stone wall.

He watched the heat shimmer in the distance and then the next thing he remembered was being cold, very cold. Slocum's eyes popped open, and he thought he had gone blind. Then he realized he had gone to sleep—passed out—sitting upright. When he had lost consciousness, he had slumped to the side, his face partially buried in the sand and rock.

He brushed away the dirt from his face and stretched, wincing in pain from his wound. He had lost more blood than he had thought. Taken along with the ride in the hot sun and the strain of dodging Jerrold and the rest of Wilson's henchmen, he had not realized how weak he was. Slocum flexed his shoulder and got his arm to feeling better. Then he tried to stand. His legs refused to obey. Crawling, he went to where he had stacked his gear, dragged out his blanket and wrapped himself in it. Within seconds he was again asleep.

This time he awoke to stifling heat. Slocum fished his watch from his pocket and stared at it, wondering if it had been broken or he had forgotten to wind it. Putting it to his ear he heard the familiar *tick-tick* and knew the time was right. Midafternoon. Of the day following his shootout with Jerrold and his two cronies. He had no sense of time passing, though his belly growled from hunger and his mouth felt like it had been stuffed with cotton wool.

He drank, ate and felt better.

"You need some water, too," he told his horse. The animal had eaten everything green within a few yards and wanted more. Especially water. As Slocum stood on shaky legs, the horse whinnied loudly and tossed its head in the direction of the charcoal kilns. Slocum worked on the hobbles, gaining strength by the minute. But when he got the hobbles free of the horse's front hooves, it bolted.

"Come back here!" he shouted, knowing the noise would only lend speed to the frightened horse's escape. But he was surprised to see the horse only ran a dozen yards, stopping to put its nose down to the ground.

Water!

Slocum joined the horse, gratefully dropping to drink from the small pond. He let the horse have its fill, then mounted. He couldn't whip his weight in wildcats, even small ones, not yet. But he felt better than he had even a half hour earlier. Slocum knew he'd need all the strength he could muster to tell Mira good-bye. But he had to do it.

It took the better part of the afternoon to make his way through the rocks and come up on the kilns from a spot where he could study the area before riding into it. Slocum used his field glasses to study every possible hiding place where Jerrold or the others might lay a trap for him. He saw nothing.

This struck him as more than a little curious. In spite of the heat, a few workers stoked the kilns, moved the charcoal from the furnaces to a packaging area, and sat around smoking hand-rolleds as they waited for the heat to do its job on the wood piles they had built all around.

Slocum checked his six-shooter and rifle, then rode down the steep gravelly slope and went to Mira's cabin. He circled it warily because it seemed preternaturally silent. Rather than call out, he dismounted, drew his gun and slowly opened the door. Mira's father, Sebastian, sat at the table in the middle of the room. He looked up with bloodshot eyes.

"What's wrong?" Slocum asked, lowering his six-shooter and then slipping it back into its holster. "Where's Mira?"

"Gone," Sebastian Van Winkle said. "They took her."

"Who? Who took her?" Slocum went cold inside anticipating Sebastian's answer.

"His name's Jerrold, and he works for Wilson. He said you'd know where to find her." Sebastian unashamedly cried. "Please, Slocum, please. Don't let them hurt my little girl!"

16

"I ain't felt this bad since Claire disappeared," Sebastian Van Winkle said. "And I'm just as helpless!" The man put his face in his hands as shudders wracked his body. Slocum pulled up a chair and sat opposite the man. Something bothered him but he couldn't put a name to it.

"Your wife?" Slocum asked. "She vanished? Mira told me she had died. I thought it was cholera or something akin."

"I lied to Mira Nell about that. I couldn't bear to tell her I didn't know what had happened to her ma. I looked, how I looked! I searched everywhere, but she was gone. No trace. I thought the Crow might have stole her away since they were on the warpath, but nobody had seen so much as a feather moving. Maybe the Indians did kidnap her, but the nearest I heard-tell of was a raid more than twenty miles off. And I looked, Slocum, and I asked and I didn't stop until I had to take care of my little girl."

"And your son. Was that about the time Rafe left you?"

Sebastian nodded and put his hands in his face again.

"Why'd they take her, Slocum? They told me they'd kill her if I tried to fetch her home. That only you was gonna be able to get her free."

"They want me," Slocum said. He described Jerrold and got Sebastian to nod assent that this was the leader of the

146

men who had taken Mira. Rocking back, Slocum sucked at his teeth as he thought.

"I've got to get her," Slocum said finally. "If I can't do it, you'll have to—"

"I'll do it!" Sebastian cried. Slocum looked at the old man. Sebastian Van Winkle had aged a decade in the span of an afternoon.

"Get Rafe. He's got plenty of men with the will riding beside him."

"What are you talking about? Rafe's gone. Like Claire."

"Not like your wife," Slocum said. "He's riding with the Mojave Guns. Don't know if you'd call him a leader, but he has a few men loyal to him."

"You're lying. My son's nowhere near Death Valley! And he's no thief! I didn't raise him to be an outlaw!"

"Believe me or not," Slocum said, getting to his feet. "It don't make me no never mind. Just remember. If I'm not back with Mira in a day, get word to the gang. Promise me."

"No, Rafe's not with a bunch of owlhoots. He couldn't be."

"He's carrying a grudge bigger than you can imagine against Big Pete Wilson. You have any idea what it is?"

"No. Wilson's a good man. Well, he was until the last week or two. He's turned mighty odd, if I can say so."

"I've noticed," Slocum said. "He'd never allow any of his men to kidnap a woman, but I have a suspicion that's what happened to Mira. Wilson told his boys to come take her."

"Slocum, you'll get her back all safe and sound, won't you?" Sebastian looked so pathetic it made Slocum a little sick. Something had broken the man's spirit or he would have put up a fight when Jerrold had kidnapped his only daughter.

Slocum left without another word. He had plans to make and a woman to rescue.

• • •

Four men guarded Mira. Slocum saw they were less than alert, but with so many posted around the small cave behind Wilson's shack, they didn't need to be wary all the time. If anything, it made getting close to Mira even harder if two or three of the guards slept in the heat because there was always a chance they might awaken, if they weren't alerted by the remaining sentry.

He might wait till night. The thought edged slowly into Slocum's mind, but he quickly discarded it. They quicker he was, the more likely he could get away with the woman. Right now, they'd be telling each other what a coward he was, how he wouldn't come for her at all and would be halfway to Mexico, a dozen lies that would lull them into thinking they were safe for the moment.

Slocum turned his binoculars to the slope above the shallow cave. A slow smile crept across his lips. There was a way to reach Mira and get out without disturbing the guards. It'd be risky, but he wasn't going to let a little thing like that stop him. Slocum grabbed his lariat and slung it over his shoulder. He winced as the rough hemp rope dragged over his exposed, injured left arm. This would slow him a mite, but Slocum was feeling stronger now and knew he could make the dangerous trip to the cave—if luck held for him.

Leaving his horse, Slocum hiked around the camp, going long miles before he reached the foot of the hill behind Wilson's shack. He finished the last of his water, then began the climb in the scorching heat to the top so he could look down on the Silver Emperor camp. He saw fewer men working than he expected. More of the miners must have either quit or been fired. Slocum wondered why any of the men still toiled for Wilson at their outrageously low wages.

He sank down to his haunches when he saw Jerrold and three more of Wilson's henchmen ride up to the mouth of the cave. They spoke in low voices with the guards, then turned and rode off in the direction of the smelter down the valley. Relatively safe from observation from below, Slocum began his hunt. It took only a few minutes to find a fissure in the top of the hill. He had noticed earlier how these crevices seemed to be everywhere throughout Wildrose Canyon. Something about the intense heat in the day and the freezing cold at night broke open the chimneys in solid rock. He flopped belly-down and peered into the depths.

He saw movement far below: Mira. In the tiny cave.

Slocum lashed his rope to a large, sturdy rock, then looped the other end around his waist. He sucked in a deep breath, knowing it was the last good air he'd get for a spell, then dropped into the crevice. For a moment he fought panic. Rock surrounded him and closed in, hot and crushingly hard. Then he forced himself to relax. This wasn't the same as the crevice leading to Herkimer and Nick— and Summers. He could look up and see the bright California sky.

Inch by inch he lowered himself, the sides of the chimney getting tighter as he went ever lower.

"Mira!" he called when he was almost at the bottom. "Mira!"

"John?"

"Anybody looking right now? Into the cave?"

He waited for what seemed an eternity, then heard a faint; "No."

Unwilling to spend a second longer than necessary in the tightness of the rock chimney, he scraped skin as he hastily lowered the remaining ten feet to the floor of the cave. First his feet popped free and then his body was no longer constrained by the rock straitjacket. He dropped to a crouch and looked up . . . at Big Pete Wilson holding a cocked and ready six-shooter.

"Figured you'd drop in, Slocum. Just never thought it'd be that literal."

"Has he harmed you, Mira?"

The woman stood behind Wilson, and behind her was the one guard Slocum couldn't spot easily from the top of the hill. Wilson hadn't taken any chances.

"No, but I'd scratch his eyes out if I get the chance!"

"You won't," Wilson said coldly. "There won't be any need if Slocum does what I tell him. I find myself in a strange position, having lost even more of my miners. I have a quota to meet and can't work the vein fast enough."

"Why do you have a quota?" Slocum asked. "You're the owner."

"No, I'm not," Wilson said bitterly. "Hearst suckered me out of it. A tiny clause in the fine print I didn't see. I'm working for him, as of a couple weeks ago. And *he* has set a quota."

"So that's why you didn't mind if all your miners walked off. It's not your mine any longer." Slocum's mind raced. More than this was explained. The four crates of silver hidden behind the shack were legally Hearst's, but Wilson had made it seem as if the Mojave Guns had stolen them. He had stolen close to $8000 worth of silver and laid the blame on outlaws. Other outlaws.

"Why not just walk away?" asked Slocum.

"I would if I could, but I can get this mine back. It's not going to pay Hearst to run it if things falls apart."

"But you've got to make it look as if you're doing everything possible to keep it producing."

"The son of a bitch might have a better lawyer than me, but I'll get the Silver Emperor back. He'll beg me to take it back!"

"Let the girl go," Slocum said. "She doesn't enter into this."

"Her brother does," Wilson said coldly. "I've been wonderin' who's got the bug up his ass to come after me the way the outlaws have. Jerrold spotted young Rafe Van Winkle. Described him just as I left him, those scars on his face and all."

"Scars? You? You did that to my brother?" Mira stared in disbelief at Wilson. "He never said how he got them." She turned to Slocum but got no support from him. "You knew, too! You knew Wilson had cut Rafe up!"

"Rafe told me," Slocum said.

"So, it's true. You and him have been, shall we say, conversing? All the better." Wilson gestured. Jerrold plucked Slocum's six-shooter from its holster.

"Can I kill him, boss?"

"Shut up," Wilson said without rancor. "Slocum is going to do some fine work for me—if he wants this young lady released unharmed. It'd be a pity to cut her up like I did her brother."

"Why'd you slice up Rafe?" asked Slocum. "He started to tell me but got interrupted."

Wilson laughed harshly. "That's between me and him. And Sebastian Van Winkle, too."

"What's my pa got to do with this? I don't understand!" Mira looked like she was at the end of her rope. She frantically paced back and forth. Slocum waited for the proper instant to jump Wilson, when Mira distracted him just right. The time never came. Wilson turned and swung his six-gun, clipping Slocum on the side of the head. Slocum stumbled and fell heavily against the cave wall.

"Don't go gettin' ideas, Slocum," Wilson said. "Jerrold, tie the bitch up. You and the boys get her—if Slocum doesn't do every little thing I want."

"What do you want in exchange for her?" Slocum asked. He didn't think it would be pretty.

"I had to pull all the smelter workers from their jobs to work the mine, and I'm still shorthanded digging the new shaft. Hearst is breathing down my neck for his damned quota, and I have to send it to him or he'll throw me out. I want you, Slocum, to sweet-talk those Injun friends of yours to come work the smelter."

"The Shoshone? They don't know jack shit about running a smelter."

"What do I care? I can show Hearst I'm trying. He can't get rid of me if there are workers. Nothing says they have to be white men."

"You want them to fail," Mira said in a hoarse whisper.

"I told you that. The Silver Emperor becomes a millstone around Hearst's neck, he gets rid of it."

Slocum knew there was more than that. Wilson had four crates of silver—and maybe more—hidden away. Hearst might have snookered him out of the mine but Wilson would walk away a rich man, even if he never got title back.

"I'll ask. Burning Tree and I aren't exactly what you'd call friends." Slocum remembered his last excursion into Shoshone territory. Any favor Burning Tree owed him had been paid in full when he had kept his fellow braves from filling Slocum with arrows.

"Get me a dozen. That ought to keep Hearst off my neck. Then," Wilson said, smirking, "then I want you to bring me Rafe Van Winkle. Him and me got a little discussin' to do."

"You want to kill him!"

"Gag her," Wilson said to Jerrold. "I'm tired of listening to her prattle. Might be, Slocum, I should cut out her tongue and let you take it to Rafe? In his mind, I've done worse."

"What does he think you did?" asked Slocum.

"Oh, he doesn't have to think I did anything. He *knows* I did." Wilson turned distant, as if remembering something from a long time back. "Wasn't my choosing things came out the way they did. But he won't ever agree. Get him here." Wilson spoke in short, clipped tones that brooked no argument.

"I'll need my six-shooter," Slocum said.

"You get it along with the girl when you've finished your chores," Wilson said. "Now get the hell out of here. I want Injuns in the smelter by noon tomorrow and Rafe Van Winkle in front of my shack by sundown."

Jerrold whistled and two guards came in. Each grabbed one of Slocum's arms and pulled him to his feet. He almost passed out from the pain of the rough treatment to his wounded arm. Then they banged his head against the ceiling, causing him to slump. The two gunmen dragged him half-conscious from the cave and set him rolling down the slope toward Wilson's shack.

"You got your orders. See to it, Slocum," Jerrold said. The burly man laughed and then said, "As much as I want to please my boss, I hope you don't bring back that little shit. I'd surely like to have a turn or two with that sweet little filly up there."

Slocum got to his hands and knees, ready to launch himself at Jerrold. He never got the chance. Jerrold was egging him on to get him into position. The kick caught Slocum smack in the middle of his chest. Stars exploded as new pain ravaged his body.

He would have passed out except that anger kept him conscious as he listened to Jerrold's mocking laughter. Slocum got to his feet and staggered away, trying to figure out how to get Mira free—and get back at Wilson and his henchmen.

17

"No firewater?" Burning Tree sat on his haunches, poking the fire with a long dry stick until the tip ignited. The Shoshone lifted the twig and watched as it burned down toward his fingers. He took no notice when ashes fell onto his skin, but Slocum saw how he tossed the burning twig down before the fire came too close.

"No firewater," Slocum said. "Mr. Wilson wants workers for the smelter. You handle fire pretty good," he said, pointing to the twig. "That's about all you have to do. Play with fire."

"Burn wood like kiln people?" Burning Tree looked at Slocum, putting him on guard. The entire discussion had been done Indian-style, not looking directly at each other.

"That's different. At the smelter, you put in rock and get silver out. It's hot and liquid, you pour it into bars and get rid of the dross—the waste rock."

"Then what do?"

"Then you start all over," Slocum said.

"What this Wilson man give Timbisha?"

Slocum considered Burning Tree's words. There was something at the charcoal kilns that interested Burning Tree that wasn't at the smelter.

"No women," Slocum said.

"Good squaw at charcoal place. Me want squaw like that."

"She's mine," Slocum said, deciding this was the best way to stifle the demand.

"You give Burning Tree? For a night?"

"No." Slocum got to his feet, thinking hard. He had to rescue Mira, but without a gun, without a dozen men at his back, without a way of getting past the gunmen Wilson had hired, such a rescue looked mighty bleak. If he tried and failed, he was likely to see Mira Nell Van Winkle dead on the ground at Jerrold's feet.

If she was lucky, all she would be was dead.

"Food," Burning Tree said suddenly. "Blankets. Guns. We want all."

"The food and blankets are good. No guns."

"Knives. We want knives."

"I'll get you knives," Slocum said. "Food, blankets, knives and perhaps a few horses." This caught Burning Tree's attention. Horses were real wealth.

"I get two horses," Burning Tree said. "He shoot at me. He chase me. Now he want Burning Tree, he pay!"

"Agreed." Slocum saw his ready acceptance of the terms of employment startled Burning Tree. The Shoshone had intended to spend the rest of the day arguing over details. That was the way of his tribe, but Slocum felt the pressure of time weighing him down. The longer Mira remained in Wilson's hands, the closer to death or dishonor she came.

"Ten? You want ten braves?"

"Each will get a horse at the end of the week, after you've worked. Food is right away. Blankets, also."

Burning Tree nodded sagely and stared into the fire, as if considering the matter. Slocum knew the lure of the horses—two for Burning Tree—was too great to pass up.

"Today. We go today," Burning Tree said.

"If you're at the smelter by sundown, I can show you what to do so you can start right away."

"We no work in dark," Burning Tree said. "Ghosts come out."

Slocum knew the Navajo worried about *chindi* roving around at night but had no idea about the Shoshone's beliefs. Burning Tree might be trying to get out of a day's work or he might be telling the truth. Slocum was too rushed to argue the matter. He agreed to this, also, again surprising the usually unflappable Indian. Slocum could read Burning Tree's mind about wanting even more, but Slocum put a quick end to such negotiation.

"Be there in one hour," he said briskly. "I'll have food and water waiting."

"No firewater?"

"No firewater," Slocum said, grinning. "I wish there was, but no firewater."

Slocum despaired when he saw how inept the Shoshones were at their smelting jobs. Such work was completely out of their experience. As odd as Slocum found it, these were hunters and farmers, not manufacturers. How anybody could get anything to grow in Death Valley was beyond him, and he had been raised by about the best farmer in all of the South. His pa was hardworking and astute and always brought in good crops. His brother Robert had the knack, and Slocum did a little, too. While he was more comfortable in the woods hunting and trapping than hoeing and harvesting, he was no tenderfoot.

So how did the Shoshone raise anything edible?

They were good hunters and raised crops in Death Valley but they knew nothing of smelting. And from their attitudes, they didn't want to learn.

"No horses, unless they get more silver bars."

"Why do you seek this shiny rock? Good for bracelets, nothing else," Burning Tree said.

"That's too complicated to explain, but you have to fill those boxes." Slocum pointed to a stack of crates.

"With shining metal?" Burning Tree sounded scornful.

The sound of hooves pounding up the trail from the mine caused Slocum to look around. He wasn't surprised to see Wilson and three of his henchmen. What worried him was that Jerrold didn't accompany Wilson. That meant Jerrold stayed at the cave to guard Mira.

"How much silver is ready to go, Slocum?"

"It's only been a couple hours," Slocum said angrily. "You can't rush smelting ore, even if you have an experienced crew."

"I need three of those boxes filled by tomorrow morning." Wilson leered at Slocum. "If I don't get them, my boys'll see about mining some silver from other mines." He made an obscene gesture showing what they would do to Mira. Slocum would have swung on Wilson but Burning Tree snickered, distracting both the mine owner and Slocum.

"I wasn't talking to you," Wilson said. The man's fists balled and he stepped toward Burning Tree. Slocum interposed himself to keep them apart.

"He's not the Indian who killed your wife. He's not even of the same tribe."

"He's a damn redskin and a redskin killed Claire."

Slocum stiffened as he stared at Wilson. The coincidence of names was too great but before he could ask after the woman, Wilson shoved him away, turned and stalked off.

"Three crates by morning, Slocum. Then you've got till sundown tomorrow to bring me Rafe Van Winkle!"

Wilson rode off in a cloud of dust that settled slowly. The still hot desert air crushed down on Slocum more than usual. He saw Burning Tree glaring at Wilson's receding back and knew the Shoshone brave wasn't likely to exhort his men to greater effort. Smelting three crates of silver in a single day might be possible with an experienced crew, but even that pushed the limits of the equipment. And nature refused to hurry when it came to the time it took to cook the ore to boil off the silver from the lead carbonate.

Burning Trees stood nearby, saying nothing as Slocum thought hard. Wilson wanted the Shoshones to fail. He wanted an excuse to pass along to George Hearst so the mining magnate would give up on the Silver Emperor

Mine. Slocum thought that wasn't likely to happen, so there had to be more to what Wilson was up to. The man had blamed the loss of a silver shipment on the Mojave Guns once. Maybe he was planning on something similar with the Indians.

Given the man's intense hatred for any Indian, it struck Slocum as plausible that Wilson would set up Burning Tree and the other Shoshones as thieves. He might have stock-piled a few crates of silver around the smelter. They would be blamed for not getting any work done—or even stealing what had been produced. Then Wilson would sneak off with the silver and be even richer at the real mine owner's expense.

"Get on back to work," Slocum said, eyeing the stacks of empty crates Wilson had ordered them to fill with silver bars. "I want to check on something."

Burning Tree grunted and went to the small knot of Shoshone behind him. He spoke rapidly for several min-utes, saying something Slocum could not interpret. He left the Indians and heaved down a crate from the stack and opened it.

A second and a third one were similarly examined.

Slocum turned and shouted to Burning Tree to join him. The Indian walked over slowly, arms crossed and stared at him, saying nothing.

"Fill up three of these boxes with ore, then stack them out where Wilson can see them."

Burning Tree scowled, then nodded once. He had no idea what was going on but this was something he and the rest of the Shoshone could do. Slocum kept looking through the crates and came to three of them at the bottom of the stack that were too heavy for him to move by him-self. He pried open the lid and stared at the contents.

In the bright Death Valley sun, he saw enough silver to make a man rich. The three crates at the bottom of the pile were already loaded—as were the ones Wilson would claim later. If Burning Tree and his friends actually pro-duced any silver, something would likely happen to those

crates, too, as they made their way to Panamint City. Or
perhaps earlier than that, Wilson would make another
switch. Wilson might have the driver stop by the charcoal
kilns to speak with George Hearst and open the boxes,
which would be mysteriously laden with rock. The
Shoshone would be blamed and Wilson could claim still
more silver.

"Not much of a crook," Slocum muttered to himself.
"He's going to be mighty surprised when the crates he
picks up are nothing but rock." Slocum put his back to
dragging a silver-laden crate away from the pile where
Wilson knew it was loaded and waiting to be picked up. He
got to an arroyo and let the box slide down to the sandy
bottom, then went to the second and third crates, sending
them after the first.

Not satisfied, Slocum loaded three more crates with
drossy rock and left them at the bottom of the stack of
empty crates. If Wilson claimed these, he would get a double dose of worthless rock. Whatever went out on the
wagon would be worthless, as would these crates.

Slocum felt little satisfaction in stacking the deck because the game still went to Wilson as long as he held Mira
prisoner.

Tired from his exertion, he flopped in the shade next to
a large water barrel, took a dipperful and drank deeply. He
poured the rest over his head to cool off and then leaned
back. He had to come up with a scheme to free Mira fast
before Wilson discovered how many crates of silver bars
had been snatched from under his nose. Somehow, Slocum
doubted Wilson was the kind who would trade the woman
for the silver, though that offer might have to be made.

Eyes growing heavy, Slocum let the heat work on him.
The sound of the Shoshone moving around inside the
smelter, doing Heaven alone knew what, lulled him and
eventually he slipped off to a light, troubled sleep.

He came awake with a start, aware that the sun was setting and that the Shoshone had stopped whatever smelting
they were up to inside. But something more caused him to

come to his feet. In the dusk moved indistinct figures, trying not to be seen as they crept along, low to the ground,
using the sparse vegetation and sandy ravines for cover.
Slocum's hand flew to his left hip, only to find an empty
holster.

Slowly backing into the smelter, he called to Burning
Tree.

"Get your men out of here. We're being attacked."

"We fight. We not children!"

"Bows and arrows against rifles and six-shooters?
There's nothing worth dying for here. Take all the food you
can, and all the blankets."

"We work for horses!"

"Take the mules. There are six in the corral out back."

"Mules? Pah!"

"Then leave them, but get the hell out of here!"

The first bullet ripped through the wall an inch above
Slocum's head. He ducked and went to the door, peering
into the twilight. The landscape had turned ominously dark
and deadly. Slocum counted four men moving closer, pistols ready. Like bees to a pollen-laden flower, they went to
the three crates Slocum had told Burning Tree to fill with
unsmelted ore. Futilely, Slocum tapped his empty holster
again.

"Got 'em? Hurry it up!" came the order in a voice
Slocum recognized well. Rafe Van Winkle led the Mojave
Guns to the source of the silver, intent on robbing the
smelter before Wilson could ship the precious bars to
Panamint City for safekeeping.

Burning Tree whispered to his braves, then they slipped
away like a shadow moving across another shadow, leaving
Slocum alone in the smelter. He peered out and saw the
outlaws bending over the crates. They grunted and cursed
and made off with the worthless crates.

Slocum couldn't fight them, and he didn't much want
to. He had other ideas. He followed the path taken by Burning Tree and his men, dashed for his horse and mounted
just as he heard loud shouts and pounding hooves. It had

taken Wilson's men a long time to figure out the outlaws were at the smelter and trying to steal the silver supposedly poured into bars that very day.

He left them to shoot it out with the Mojave Guns and headed up the canyon toward the Silver Emperor Mine—and Mira Van Winkle. Slocum knew it was now or never if he wanted to free her.

18

Slocum rode through the darkness, letting his horse pick its way on the rocky slope. He had little hope of rescuing Mira, but he had to try. More than once his hand went to the empty holster, then he forced himself to stop thinking of the missing Colt Navy. Whatever he did had to rely on brains, not firepower.

He got to the edge of the camp with gunfire still ringing in his ears from the fight going on at the smelter. Slocum hit the ground and walked his horse to avoid being too noticeable. It was lucky on his part because one shift from the mine was coming off and another trudging to their work. He heard the tired grumbles of the miners, most of them vowing to quit as soon as Wilson paid them their due. Slocum kept his head down and avoided contact.

How he wanted to tell them Wilson wasn't likely to pay them even the pittance they toiled for! Wilson had said he wanted his mine back from the legal maneuvering of George Hearst, but it looked increasingly as if Wilson simply wanted to plunder what he could. He made the gang of road agents look like pikers with his crates of silver hidden behind his shack, not to mention the ones he had tried to steal from the smelter. Slocum wondered how many more Wilson had tucked away for safekeeping, blaming their loss on road agents or Indians.

Slocum kept walking as the miners went into the mess hall for food. He noted that they were working shifts of twelve hours on, twelve hours off, enough to kill most men. But they only complained and nothing more as they burrowed into the hillside to create a new mine. Slocum considered blowing up the mine again as retribution for Wilson kidnapping Mira, but he quickly pushed aside that notion. Men worked inside all the time now to give Wilson as much silver as possible to steal.

Slocum fed and watered his horse at the company barn, then sat on a hay bale to think through his problems. Getting Mira free was paramount. He wondered what George Hearst might say about Big Pete Wilson kidnapping and stealing the way he had. Although Mira worked for Hearst at the charcoal kilns, Slocum doubted the mining magnate would be too upset over losing her or anyone else in his employ. Any man who stole a producing silver mine from another wasn't likely to care much about the people working for him. No, if Slocum went to Hearst it had to be with proof that Wilson was stealing the silver—and possibly how Wilson was trying to get his mine back, by force of arms if necessary. Why else hire so many gunfighters and so few miners and smelter workers?

None of those tidbits of information were likely to spur George Hearst to action. And even if Slocum located him, it might take days to drop the noose around Wilson's neck. By then Mira could be dead and Wilson halfway to Mexico.

Slocum had to admit Wilson had been cagey in everything he did. Slocum stood to take the blame for most all the theft because he was foreman. The Shoshone working at the smelter could be blamed for part of the theft—and who had hired them? John Slocum. The only silver lining Slocum saw to that debacle was hiding three crates of silver bars at the smelter where Wilson wasn't likely to stumble across them. But if he sent his henchmen out to scour the countryside, they would find the crates eventually.

Slocum got to his feet and edged into the dark barn, hunting for a weapon. He had never seen a rifle or shotgun stored in there, and he didn't find any now. The best he could uncover was a broken ax handle hidden under a pile of straw in a horse stall. He hefted it. It felt good slamming into his palm. It would feel even better if he brought it down on top of Jerrold's ugly skull.

Armed with the club, Slocum went outside and got his bearings, then headed toward Wilson's shack with the intent of clobbering Jerrold and saving Mira. He had hardly gone a dozen paces when he heard someone coming up fast behind him.

"Don't bother turning, Slocum," Wilson said. "I've got you covered with a shotgun. Throw down that stick."

Slocum dropped the ax handle and stared ahead along the dark path.

"How'd you figure I'd be here?" Slocum had to ask.

"I put a string tied to a tin can across the path. You set off my alarm, I came out and sure as sin, there you were."

Slocum cursed himself. He was tired, still a bit woozy from the cut on his arm and had gotten careless. Such a simple tripwire ought to have been easily seen and avoided.

"What're you going to do now?"

"You haven't finished your chores for me," Wilson said. "My men made the mistake of chasing after the outlaws when they tried to rob the silver from the smelter. 'Bout the only guards I have left are Jerrold and a couple of his friends."

Slocum cursed under his breath. He should have been more careful, and he would have succeeded in freeing Mira.

"You offer too big a reward for the outlaws?"

"Something like that," Wilson said in disgust. "I should have believed in your abilities. You keep surprising me with how well you deliver the goods."

"Like the Shoshone workers at the smelter?"

Wilson laughed. "Fabulous! They were so inept! I told Hearst they were stealing us—him—blind and he bought it." Wilson sobered a little. "That's why the rewards are so high for the outlaws. Anybody stealing from the smelter's got a hundred-dollar reward on their heads."

"That makes your head mighty valuable," Slocum said.

"Shut your pie hole!" snapped Wilson. "I've got to tie up some loose ends."

"So that means there's no way you'll get the Silver Emperor back from Hearst?"

"The son of a bitch sewed up the contract tighter 'n I thought. I have to pay off a mountain of debt before I can even think of buying it back. And even with low output, he's asking a fortune."

"What happened that you lost the mine?" asked Slocum. He winced when Wilson poked him in the back with the shotgun muzzle to get him moving along the rocky path leading to the cave where Mira was being held.

"I should have been content with the Silver Emperor but another deal came up. I bought too damned much of a worthless hole in the ground."

"And Hearst loaned you the money, using the Silver Emperor as collateral."

"He's a devil. Stealing from him ought to be a ticket straight to Heaven."

Wilson shoved Slocum forward again, and he stumbled into the mouth of the cave. From either side came dark figures. One was the hulking Jerrold. The other was a smaller gunman Slocum had seen earlier.

"I need him kept on ice for the night. In the morning, Slocum's going to track down Rafe Van Winkle for me."

"Why'd I do that?"

"You think more of his sister than you do him, that's why," Wilson said. "I got a score to settle with him. Don't much care about her."

"What are you going to do to Rafe?"

"You probably came from the camp. Maybe even put your horse in the barn. Did you see the beam outside the hayloft? I replaced the pulley with a noose. You get Van Winkle back here and I'm gonna string him up, just as he deserves."

"Then what'll you do? Hightail it with—" Slocum staggered forward when intense pain went pinwheeling through his head. Wilson had slugged him before he could reveal the man's plans to Jerrold and his partner. That told Slocum more than anything Wilson could have spoken out loud. Wilson played a solitary hand.

"Push a big rock across the opening," Wilson ordered Jerrold. "No talkin' to him. You do and I'll string you up alongside Rafe Van Winkle, when Slocum finds him."

Slocum didn't hear Jerrold's answer, but a large boulder was rolled across the opening, blocking what light came from the stars and plunging the cave to almost total darkness.

"Mira?" he called. "Where are you?"

He began feeling his way toward the rear of the shallow cave. At first his fingers touched only rock. Then he found something warm and soft and shapely.

"Umm, that's about the nicest thing I've felt crawling up my leg since they put me in here," Mira said softly. "Why don't you keep exploring? You might find something you like. And something I'd like for you to find, too."

Slocum had to laugh. Even in their predicament, Mira had a sense of humor—and something more. He ran his hand up a bit farther and knew he stroked over her thigh. But this was no time to be fooling around. Or was it?

He thought about it for a moment. There wasn't much chance he was going to escape, not with the rock blocking the mouth of the cave and Jerrold and his partner standing guard. Wilson wasn't far off, probably guarding his crates of silver bars. If he and Mira were here until dawn, without any chance of escape, why not enjoy their time together?

Slocum turned a bit more glum when he realized this might be their last time together. Wilson wasn't likely to let anybody live after he had strung up Rafe, not if he figured to hightail it out of the territory with crates of silver that rightly belonged to another man.

"You've stopped," Mira accused. "Aren't you interested in seeing what's even higher?" She wiggled a little and scooted down so the back of his hand brushed against a fleecy patch. When she felt it, she clamped her legs together, trapping his hand in place.

"I'm interested in doing some exploring," Slocum said.

"You've already been in that cave. Maybe that's taking away the thrill?" she suggested. Mira rocked to and fro, his trapped hand rubbing against her nether lips.

"Not too interested in exploring anywhere else," Slocum told her.

"That's good. I wouldn't like it too much if you went farther afield for your fun."

Slocum blinked and tried to see her, but the darkness was absolute. He looked up and thought he saw a faint star at the very top of the crevice he had descended before. His heart jumped, thinking how he might wiggle his way back up that chimney. Then Slocum faced reality. He had almost no chance of making it up the narrow crevice with his arm hurting like it was, and even if he did, Wilson probably had a guard posted at the top who would be alerted by scraping sounds long before Slocum could pop up and out.

Slocum suddenly realized something else was popping up and out. He hadn't see or felt her moving, but Mira had contrived to swing around, keeping his right hand pinned so delightfully, and bring her hands to his belt. Slocum felt her nimble fingers working to unfasten his jeans and tease out his hardened manhood. For a moment, his rock-hard shaft swung free in the air. Then he gasped as he felt hot lips close on the very top.

He moaned as she began running her tongue all over the tip, stroking and licking and kissing as she went. From the blunt end Mira worked down the thick stalk to the base where her lips opened and she took the hairy sac entirely into her mouth. As she pressed her tongue against him and gently gnawed on her unearthed treasure, Slocum almost lost control. Every time her wet tongue lashed out, he felt a lightning bolt lance through his loins.

He decided to give as good as he was getting. He slid his hand around a bit and finally wormed a finger into her heated interior where he wiggled it about. This caused Mira to momentarily abandon her oral post. Slocum rolled over and came to hands and knees, with the woman under him. She reached up and stroked over his length, tugging gently to pull it back to her mouth.

Slocum slid his finger from her wet, warm interior and stroked up the sides of her bare thighs, pushing her skirt up around her waist to fully expose her crotch—if he could only see it. He dropped down, blindly hunting for the spot where his finger had roamed so eagerly a few seconds before. His chin touched her belly. Slocum toyed with her pleasurably, dragging his stubbled chin over her sleek, smooth belly before moving lower now that he had the range.

His lips touched the tangled mat nestled between her legs at the same time she sucked on his hardness and drew him back into her mouth. Slocum burrowed down a little more and sent his tongue to reaming her out just as she was giving him such a good tongue lashing. He tasted the well of her being, his tongue swirling around the rim before sinking back in. Mira gasped and sobbed and then went back to giving him the same pleasure he was giving her.

Their mutual oral explorations grew more intense. Slocum's lips brushed over a tiny spire of flesh at the juncture of her soft, pink, scalloped gates protecting her innards. He sucked it into his mouth and lightly flicked his tongue over the tip. Mira's back arched as she tried to cram her crotch fully into his face.

Slocum lost his position and had to hunt about as excitement rippled through the woman's tensed, yearning body. He drove his tongue deeply into her and wiggled it around, sampling her womanly wines, then retreated. Slocum found it increasingly hard to concentrate on what he was doing because of the sensations building like flood waters behind a dam at his own crotch.

He ran his hands around outside Mira's legs and drew her hips up to better lick and kiss. But when she shrieked in release, her legs thrust out straight, he lost his grip on them.

"Are you all right?" he asked. The darkness prevented him from seeing her face to judge her condition.

"Never been better," she said, heaving a deep sigh. "But I want more, John. If we have to while away the hours, I want you to *really* while me!"

"Is that what they're calling it now?" he said, laughing.

"I don't care what you call it," Mira said. He felt her hot breath in his ear, followed by her questing tongue. Then she kissed across the stubble on his chin and finally found his lips. Their kiss turned more passionate as Mira moved about, straddling Slocum's waist. He moved back enough to sit up and brace himself against the cave wall. It was a good thing Slocum had something solid behind him because Mira lowered her hips over his lap. The tip of his rigid shaft touched those lips he had kissed so intimately, then it vanished within the woman's clinging, heated, excitingly tight orifice.

A shudder passed through both of them as Mira settled down.

"I want more," she said, her voice shaking with desire. "Go on, open my blouse. You know what to do."

"Wish I could see what I'm doing."

He fumbled at the buttons holding Mira's blouse closed, but she had other ideas. She jerked away from him, sending the buttons flying into the dark. He heard the pearl buttons rattling against stone and then only silence—silence and harsh breathing as Mira anticipated what his mouth might do now. Slocum didn't keep her guessing. He bent over and kissed the top of one breast, then hastily moved to the other. Back and forth his lips flew until he took one of the hardened nubs between his lips and suckled for all he was worth. A new tremor passed through Mira, giving her yet another intense release. He pressed down on the rubbery flesh capping her breast and felt it turning even harder as blood pumped furiously into it, driven by her racing heart. He gnawed and tongued and used his teeth against the tender nipple. Then he buried his face between the mountains of her breasts.

Mira pushed herself forward as he turned and licked the insides of her tender mounds. Slocum added to the woman's arousal by running his hands up and down over her bare thighs and finally around to cup the fleshy cheeks of her rump. With his strong hands he squeezed down and began kneading the handfuls of her behind as if the two half moons were lumps of pliant dough. He discovered there was the added benefit of giving Mira such stimulation. As he pressed her ass cheeks together, it tightened her already narrow female sheath around his hidden length.

"Yes, oh, my whole body's on fire, John. I . . . I . . . aieee!"

Slocum set off her tumultuous emotional release again. This time he found it impossible to hold back his own needs and desires. He clutched her firmly around the waist and lifted her trim body just enough for her to slip free and engulf only the purpled arrowhead at the end of his manstalk. Then Slocum released her. Mira sagged down, taking him fully within her clinging interior.

She got the idea of what he wanted—and she obviously wanted it for herself, also. Slocum's hands drifted from her waist and cupped her breasts. With a double handful of firm but malleable flesh, he guided her in an up-and-down motion that set a bonfire in his loins.

"Oh, you fill me up so, John," she gasped out. Slocum felt the sweat pouring from her and licked and suckled and tried to keep from exploding like some young buck with his first woman. But Mira's skills were too great, her need matching his own. She tensed her strong inner muscles and clamped down around him, then released slowly, agonizingly slowly. And then she rushed back, twisted and turned with him fully within, and rose.

The fire spread throughout Slocum's body, and he exploded in a wild release that almost took the top off his head. All too soon he began to melt like snow in the Death Valley heat and Mira sagged forward, her cheek pressing into his chest.

"What now, John?"

"No more, for the time being," he said, panting harshly. His shirt was plastered to his body from the sweat of their active lovemaking.

"That's not what I meant," Mira said. "What are we going to do to get out of here, now that we've had our little fun."

"It wasn't so little for me, nor for you, 'less I miss my guess."

"You know what I mean, silly," she said, moving away. She hiked a leg up and swung around to sit next to him. She rested her head on his shoulder. Slocum still couldn't see her in the absolute darkness of the cave and wished he could. Depending on Wilson's mood, this might be the last time they'd have a chance to look at one another.

"He wants me to track down Rafe. I can find him and see if your brother won't throw in with me to free you."

"Wilson must know you'd think of that. He's got something else in mind. He's a cunning son of a bitch," she said with venom.

Slocum stroked her hair as he thought. Mira was right. Even if Slocum found Rafe, it wasn't right to bring him back for Wilson to string up like a chicken waiting to be gutted. As long as the mine owner—former mine owner— held Mira captive, he had the ace in this desperate game.

"What's that?" Mira jerked upright. "Did you hear it?"

Slocum was already on his feet, using his hand to guide himself to a point where he could look up into the crevice. He saw a shadow moving up there, occasionally blocking the few stars visible.

"Who's up there?" he called. Slocum worried that Jerrold would laugh at him or drop a stone on his head to taunt him. Then he heard words he did not understand—but he recognized the language.

"Burning Tree!"

"You prisoner?"

"Can you get us out?"

"Squaw with you?"

"Yes," Slocum said, he waved his hand to silence Mira's

outraged outburst, but she couldn't see him the dark. He had to quiet her. "Can you get us both out? I'll make it worth your while."

"What you give Burning Tree?"

"All the horses in the corral at the mine, all of them but mine and one other," Slocum said.

"Me take anyhow."

Slocum knew better than to offer silver to the Shoshone. To the Indians it was only a decorative metal, not worth dying for.

"We're friends, you and me," Slocum said. "Friends will get friends out of trouble."

"Oh, right, that's going to convince him," muttered Mira. Slocum's anger flared, not because of her cynicism but because she was right. But he had nothing more to offer the Shoshones for their help.

"Burning Tree!" Slocum called. "Burning Tree!"

Silence. Slocum peered up and saw the handful of stars through the fissure and knew the Indian had left. He sucked in a deep breath and exhaled. He was in a fix and didn't know how he was going to get out, much less save Mira.

Slocum swung around and found Mira in his arms, clinging fiercely to him. Her tears added to the moisture on his shirt. They sank to the floor and stayed like that for the rest of the night, Slocum's frustration at his helplessness grew throughout the night until he wanted to rage against such an unlucky turn of fate that had brought him to the Silver Emperor Mine in the first place.

After an eternity in the darkness, the rock blocking the cave mouth grated away and let in the pale dawn of a new day. From the smirk on Big Pete Wilson's face it wasn't going to be a good day for John Slocum.

19

Slocum squinted and moved to put himself between Mira and the shotgun levelled in Wilson's hands.

"Come on out and greet the fine new day, Slocum. You, too, Miss Van Winkle. I got a real surprise for you two."

"What is it?" Mira asked anxiously. Slocum wanted to silence her. Giving Wilson even a hint of pleasure at her apprehension was more than the man deserved. He fed on such fear and uncertainly like a buzzard ripped away dead flesh with its beak.

"Glad you asked," Wilson said, motioning with the shotgun for them to leave their rocky prison. "I was gonna have Slocum ride out to find your brother, but it turned out I don't have to do that. My boys might have gotten all het up and chased those road agents all over Death Valley, but they caught themselves the one I wanted most."

"You've got Rafe?" Mira gasped and put her hand to her mouth. She turned from Wilson, who laughed in delight at her upset.

"They caught him, and I already gave 'em their reward. In fact, four of them caught him so I gave each of 'em a hundred dollars. In silver."

Slocum started to ask if it came from the stash behind the shack, but he held his angry words. Telling Wilson that he knew of that particular theft from the real mine owner

173

only spelled a one-way ticket to a grave. Wilson might not even bother digging a grave. He might cut Slocum in half with that scattergun and just roll the rock back. Slocum's knowledge of the hidden silver was his only trump card, but he had to wait until the right time to play it.

If he even got into the game. It looked bleaker by the minute that he or Mira—much less Rafe Van Winkle— would ride away from the Silver Emperor. Slocum and Mira silently obeyed as Wilson motioned for them to go down the slope toward the bunkhouses and the barn.

As Slocum approached, he went cold inside. The noose dangling from the hayloft brace was ominously empty, but the tight knot of gunmen just under it boded ill. As Wilson and his two prisoners got closer, the gunmen stepped back, showing a battered Rafe Van Winkle. He had been worked over pretty well when Wilson's men caught him. One eye was swelled shut, and his face was puffy and covered with purpled bruises. His hands were tied behind his back and he stood on one leg, favoring the other. Slocum saw the left pants leg was torn and soaked with blood. Rafe had put up a hell of a fight but had been overwhelmed by too many men.

Would the rest of the Mojave Guns come to save one of their own? Slocum doubted it. There was no loyalty among road agents. They were ornery sons of bitches who drifted together and decided to enrich themselves and devil take the hindmost. Slocum almost wished the gang was more like the James or Doolin-Dalton gangs where most of the members were either related or lifelong friends. That would be the only reason the rest of the Mojave Guns would come for Rafe.

Looking around, Slocum reckoned he saw all of Rafe's kin. Mira brushed Slocum's shoulder as they walked closer to the lynch mob and a wide-eyed Sebastian Van Winkle stared fixedly at his son. Slocum could only wonder at the shock Sebastian felt at seeing Rafe after all this time.

Or was it so much of a shock? Slocum had the feeling father and son lied to themselves a great deal about what went on between them.

"Make a fuss," Slocum whispered to Mira. "If we don't get out now, we'll never get away alive."

Mira showed no sign of hearing but she let out a screech, pushed past a couple gunmen and tried to throw her arms around her brother's neck. She was screaming and crying and then began kicking and biting when two of Wilson's henchmen tried to pull her away from Rafe.

Slocum ducked, feinted left and drove right, his shoulder digging into a gunman's rib cage. But his fight amounted to nothing. Wilson had been watching and thrust out his foot, tripping Slocum. As Slocum got to his knees, he felt the large bores of a double-barreled shotgun thrust against his ear.

"Reckoned you'd try something foolish, Slocum. That's the kind of man you are. Foolish!" Wilson swung the shotgun and clipped Slocum on the side of the head, stunning him. In the distance, through the roar in his ears, Slocum heard Wilson say to Jerrold, "Keep a gun trained on him all the time. Drill him if he tries anything."

"What then, boss?"

"We'll see to them after that one's hanged."

Slocum didn't have to know that Wilson pointed at Rafe. Not looking in the direction he launched himself, Slocum lashed out trying to create more disturbance. Jerrold wasn't caught unawares as Slocum had hoped. The man laughed cruelly and kicked Slocum to the ground, then started to shoot him. Slocum looked up into Jerrold's six-shooter, but Wilson stopped him.

"Later, I said later."

"Git to yer feet, Slocum. 'Less you want to die down there in the dust with the rest of the insects."

Slocum got to his feet, still looking for something to give him an edge. It looked as if the hanging was going to happen, and there wasn't anything Slocum could do except watch.

"Get a horse and bring it over. Let our guest of honor feel the hemp around his neck for a minute or two 'fore you give that ole horse a swat on the rump."

"I didn't expect any better from you, Wilson," Rafe

called as men hoisted him to the horse. "Not after you stole away my ma!"

Silence fell and for a moment it looked as if everyone had been caught in a sudden freeze.

"What're you saying, Rafe?" Sebastian Van Winkle pulled free of the men holding him and stepped closer.

"You're dumber 'n a bag of nails, Pa," Rafe said. His scars turned bright pink and turned his cheek to a checkerboard in the rising sun. "He lured Ma away. He sweet-talked her away from us, and you didn't do anything."

"I didn't have to do much sweet-talking," Wilson said. Slocum saw how grim Wilson had become. "Claire was already carryin' my baby when she went off with me."

"You killed her!" cried Rafe. "You murdered her!"

"The Crow killed her. They killed Claire and our unborn child." Wilson's hands shook as he clutched the shotgun so hard that his knuckles turned white. Slocum wondered if Wilson would lift it and shoot Rafe from the saddle rather than hang him.

"You and Claire?" Sebastian Van Winkle stared. His mouth moved but no more words came out.

"You're lying!" shouted Mira. But Slocum wondered who she was calling out as a liar. Somehow, Slocum thought they were all telling the truth, from the way they saw it. Claire Van Winkle had fooled around with Wilson behind her husband's back, then run off with him only to be slaughtered by Indians. Sebastian had spent the rest of his life denying it—and his son had vowed revenge.

"How'd Rafe come by those scars?" Slocum asked.

"He tried to murder me one night while I was sleeping in my bedroll, but I was too smart for him. I caught him and cut him up a little to scare some sense into him. He wouldn't believe his ma went with me willingly or that she was already knocked up with what I hoped would be his half-brother, that his old man was a fool Claire couldn't tolerate even one more day. She chose and she chose me! Rafe couldn't believe that, but he could believe the pain I gave him. And now I'm gonna give him one last dose of pain that'll break his damned neck!"

Slocum heard the hatred boiling in Wilson's words. It matched what he'd already heard from Rafe. The two men ought to have been locked in a room and only the survivor let out. Slocum scowled at this thought. There wouldn't be any need for such a blood fight in a few more seconds. Rafe would be kicking his heels for the last time as soon as Wilson whacked the mare's rump and sent it running.

"You're lying," Mira said. "My ma never left with you. Not when you . . . you . . ." The woman sputtered and couldn't go on.

"Why'd Claire want you and not me, not her own children?" Sebastian Van Winkle croaked.

"You know the answer to that better 'n anybody but Claire," Wilson said. "Tell you what, Sebastian. I'm gonna do you a favor. I'm gonna let you get that nag moving. The one your son's sittin' on!"

"No, no," Sebastian shook his head but the men on either arm held him firmly.

"Why not? You drove off Claire with your drinking and abuse, and from all I can tell, you set your own boy out to do what any other man'd consider his own duty."

"I never even knew you! I never saw you 'til I came to Death Valley to work in the kilns!"

"You never knew," taunted Wilson. "You never knew about me." Wilson laughed harshly, almost maniacally. "Enough of this. Give that horse's ass a good swat, Sebastian. Do it or I swear you'll have to watch what my boys do to your daughter!"

"Pa!" Mira struggled. Like her father she was held too securely to get away.

Slocum looked from them to where Jerrold climbed onto a barrel to put the noose around Rafe's neck. He braced himself for the moment when all eyes would be on Rafe's last instant on this earth. Only then might he get free, get a pistol, get away.

Then all hell broke loose. A huge explosion rocked the ground and everyone turned toward the smelter. Flames thirty feet high licked at the hot desert sky.

Wilson's men stared in stunned silence, giving Slocum the change to jerk free and grab Wilson's shotgun. The horse under Rafe reared, pawed the air and then tore off, frightened at the commotion. Slocum cut loose with both barrels, tearing through most of the rope above Rafe's head. For a frightening instant, Slocum thought Rafe was going to die, not of a broken neck but from strangulation. Then the uncut portion of the hemp gave way under the man's weight, letting him crash to the ground.

"Get them. Kill them Injuns!" shrieked Wilson. His eyes were wide and he ran about, waving his arms and adding to the confusion rather than rallying his men for a more effective fight.

Slocum looked around and saw Burning Tree and a dozen other Shoshones racing up from the smelter. Burning Tree had set fire to it and created the diversion Slocum needed. Now the Shoshones swarmed over the corral, stealing all the horses and mules they could find. Wilson's henchmen fired a few times but seeing the onslaught of armed Indians, quickly turned tail and ran, diving for cover and trying not to be seen as they went.

Slocum waded into the fray, swinging the empty shotgun and fighting his way to Rafe Van Winkle. Using both hands on the shotgun stock, Slocum swung the weapon and connected squarely with Jerrold's head. The burly gunman straightened, his eyes rolled up into his head and then he fell like tall timber cut down by a lumberjack.

"G-get it off. Chokin' me somethin' fierce," Rafe grated out. Slocum hastily loosened the rope and let the man breathe again. Then he unfastened the bindings around Rafe's wrists.

"See to your pa," Slocum said. "I think he's hurting." Slocum couldn't tell if Sebastian Van Winkle had been injured or if the shock of everything he had heard affected him most. He simply sat on a bale of hay and stared off into the distance.

"Where's Mira Nell?" asked Rafe.

"I'll see to her," Slocum said. He grabbed the six-shooter from Jerrold's flaccid grip and felt better. At the sound of a war whoop, he turned and saw Burning Tree with his warriors rounding up the horses from the corral. They had let the mules go free to mill about and cause even more confusion.

Slocum waved and grinned when he saw that Burning Tree had done as Slocum had asked. All the horses were taken from the corral—all but Slocum's. The Shoshones rode off whooping and hollering. Slocum wished he could ride with them, but he had one more chore to finish.

He looked around and saw Mira disappearing up the trail leading back to Wilson's shack. Tearing after her, he hoped he wouldn't be too late. Wilson was a cornered rat now and all the more dangerous. Slocum skidded to a halt a dozen yards away when he saw that Wilson had trapped Mira and held her to the ground, a knife at her throat. But the woman wasn't frightened. She was belligerent.

"Why'd you let my pa and me work at the kilns? You knew what you'd done with my ma."

"It amused me," Wilson said. "There you and him were, not knowing." Wilson's shoulders slumped a little at the memory of what he had lost. Slocum lifted the six-gun, but the range was long for a shot that wouldn't also endanger Mira. "It amused me that Sebastian was there and didn't know. And I see so much of Claire in you. You look like her."

Slocum fired. The bullet ripped painfully across Wilson's shoulders, causing him to lose his balance. The knife he had intended to plunge into Mira's throat went instead into the ground. Slocum fired a second time. This round caught Wilson in the side of the head, killing him instantly.

"Damn you, John! I wanted to kill him. I wanted to kill him. I wanted to!" Mira rolled over and hid her face in her hands, deep sobs racking her body.

Slocum didn't bother pointing out she'd never have had the chance. What the truth actually was had died with Wilson. And Slocum found himself not really caring.

"Come on, let's go into the cabin where you can sit down."

"I want his scalp! That's what the Indians do. I want his damned scalp!" Mira fought but Slocum held her firmly, guiding her toward the shack. Inside she collapsed on the bed, still crying her eyes out. Slocum rummaged around and found a bottle of whiskey, poured himself a shot and downed it, then poured one for Mira.

"Drink this," he ordered. "It'll calm you down a mite."

"I wanted to kill him for all he'd done. What an evil man!"

"Reckon so," Slocum said, taking another shot. He let the warmth spread through his belly and body. Too many more drinks and he'd be drunk. He couldn't remember the last time he'd eaten or had anything else liquid to wet his whistle.

He swung the six-shooter around when the door flew open. Rafe Van Winkle filled the doorway with his broad shoulders.

"Come on in and have a drink," Slocum said, pushing the bottle in Rafe's direction. "Don't worry about Mira. She'll be all right when she calms down."

"He's dead. I saw the body. You do it?" Rafe glared at Slocum.

"Let me guess. You wanted to kill him. Well, so did your sister. I beat you to it." Slocum didn't care any more if he got drunk. He took another stiff belt and felt better for it. "How's your pa?"

"I don't know. He just stares off into space. Something happened to his mind. That doctor from the mine's looking at him."

"Doc Lonigan," said Slocum. He shrugged. Lonigan wasn't a doctor but would be better for what ailed Van Winkle right now than either of his children.

"Yeah, that's him. The other miners showed up after

Wilson's goons were gone." Rafe sounded tired but his eyes were still wide and he had a crazed look about him. Slocum wondered if that was better than Mira crying furiously on the bed. Or their father simply checking out and going somewhere nobody could touch him again.

"We ain't nobody's fools," said Herkimer from the doorway. "When them boys showed up with the outlaw—this here young'n—we all decided it wasn't worth gettin' our heads blowed off."

"Herk, I need a word with you," Slocum said. Slocum spun and faced Rafe, saying, "You and your sister stay here." When the young outlaw ignored him, he pushed Rafe into a chair. The man tried to fight but saw the cold determination in Slocum's eyes and settled down. "Look after her. I'll be back in a few minutes."

"Man alive, Slocum, this is 'bout the most—" Herkimer began. He clamped his mouth shut when Slocum turned his cold stare on him.

"This way. I got something to show you." Slocum led the way upslope to where Wilson had cached the silver. He pulled away the tarp, then pried open a lid to reveal the treasure trove.

"Don't that beat all," Herkimer said slowly. "Why'd Mr. Wilson stash it here?"

"He was stealing it. He lost title to the mine to George Hearst and was stealing from the new owner." Slocum heaved a sigh. "Nobody but you and me know this is here," Slocum said. He looked at the expectant miner and went on. "Four crates of silver, split between the miners, ought to pay them off for everything they've put up with these past months."

"You'll take a cut, won't you, Slocum?"

"It's all yours, you and the rest of the men. Four crates worth." Slocum saw the greed flare in Herkimer's eyes.

"Don't seem right, you not takin' anything."

"I'll take my horse," Slocum said. "And I'll take the Van Winkles back to the smelter."

"Been over there after the Injuns set it on fire. Ain't

much of anything left, 'less you like lookin' at charcoal."
Herkimer laughed. "But then, I reckon they do."

"Wait until we've gone before you get the men up here.
You might bury Wilson first, though why is beyond me."

"You're quite a man, Slocum. Thank you."

Slocum shook hands with Herkimer, then called to Rafe
and Mira to come with him. They walked down the slope to
where Sebastian Van Winkle sat quietly. Lonigan shook his
head.

"Can't figure anything to do for him, Slocum. I've seen
this kind of behavior before but the gent in question had
been kicked in the head by a horse."

"About the same, except Sebastian got kicked in the
heart," Slocum said. He turned and took Rafe and Mira
aside.

"No, John, let me tend him. I can help. Let me," said
Mira, struggling to pull free of his grip.

"He's not going anywhere," Slocum said. "I want to tell
you about some silver that might help you out."

"The crates up there?" Rafe jerked his thumb over his
shoulder. "The silver you gave to the miners?"

"Wilson stole it. But then that doesn't bother you much,
does it?"

Rafe looked defiantly at Slocum and gave all the answer
he needed.

"Wilson's paid for what he did to your family," Slocum
said. "But he can pay just a tad more. There're three crates
of silver in an arroyo by the smelter. Take it. All yours.
That's not pay for what Wilson did but it'll help find help
for your pa, maybe in San Francisco or over in Denver.
South of Denver at Manitou Springs there's a spa where he
might take the waters and recover."

Slocum looked at Mira, wanting to ask her to ride with
him. But she hardly listened. She stared at her father.

"You take good care of him," Slocum said.

"Yes, yes, John. We will." Mira hurried to sit beside Sebastian Van Winkle and hold his hand.

"It's not enough," Rafe said.

Slocum spun, grabbed the man's shirt and lifted him onto his toes. "Listen good," he said. "Hate will eat you up if you let it. You were about the worst road agent I ever saw. Go back to it and you'll swing from some judge's gallows. Take the silver and make a new life for yourself, your sister and your pa. Try to find some new outrage to avenge and you're going to be dead within a year."

Slocum let Rafe down. The hatred still bubbled and boiled in the young man, but Slocum thought he saw a glimmer of good sense rising to the top. He turned and almost went to Mira, to ask if she wanted to ride with him, then changed his mind. She was as obsessed as her brother and would need time to work her way out of the tangled skein of memory and guilt.

He walked briskly to the barn, fetched his horse, mounted and rode out, tipping his hat to Mira Nell as he left—to ride to the smelter. There was no good reason for the Van Winkles to have all the silver he had hidden there. With saddlebags full of the shining metal, Slocum could ride long and far and maybe forget everything that had happened in Death Valley at the Silver Emperor Mine.

Maybe.

Watch for

SLOCUM AND THE TWO GOLD BULLETS

324th novel in the exciting SLOCUM series
from Jove

Coming in February!

Explore the exciting Old West with one of the men who made it wild!

J. R. ROBERTS

THE GUNSMITH